SPIRIT SISTER,
I SING YOUR SONG

Patricia Jacobs

SPIRIT SISTER, I SING YOUR SONG
Written by Patricia Jacobs
Copyright © 2015 Patricia Jacobs

This is a work of fiction. Names, characters, places, and incidents are either the product of the author's imagination or are used fictitiously. The Akwanakai is a fictitious representation of the many pre-European Great Lakes Native American tribes, their culture, customs, and spirituality. Any resemblance to actual persons, living or dead, events, locales, or tribes is entirely coincidental.

Published by PageBreak Press of Chicago

Art work: Indie Designz

ISBN: 978-0-9966951-0-7

Cataloguing Information:
Jacobs, Patricia
Spirit Sister, I Sing Your Song
2015
Fiction—teen/ young adult—fantasy—time travel
Native American—historical fiction

DEDICATION

To my husband Gary who through his encouragement, love, and input made a dream possible. And to my children: Brian, Lynnette, Mark, Christopher and Annalisa.

ACKNOWLEDGEMENTS

My daughter Annalisa and her friends Pamela and Rachel. When in high school they were my first beta readers. Their time, encouragement, and enthusiasm motivated me to keep writing.

My dear friend and "Spirit Sister" Annette. She enabled me to resume writing at a time when life and will power had collapsed.

Mary Ellen who read my manuscript to her classes three years in succession and provided the invaluable feedback of her students.

Myles Goddard for reading an early draft of my novel and offering suggestions for cultural accuracy.

And family and friends who read the novel and provided encouragement.

Prologue

A little girl cocked her head and giggled into her older sister's shoulder.

"Ah, little chipmunk," Grandmother said, "tell me what you are thinking."

"Oldest Grandmother, you are wise above all others. When I, too, can speak words that no one can understand, will I be also wise like you?'

The old woman gave a merry laugh as she surveyed the children's puzzled faces. "I can see you think I speak in strange riddles. Yes, I have told of being born into one life and then journeying here to my true people. That is yet a riddle, even to me."

The fierce wind and snow of the Hunger Moon was an angry bear roaring and clawing at the wigwam. The flames of the fire spit and crackled, casting eerie, dancing shadows on the bark walls.

Huddled under fur robes, with little brown faces wide-eyed and mouths agape, the children sat cross-legged in a semi-circle before the old woman. Thin white braids framed her brown face, its skin the texture of crepe paper. Her knobby fingers, seldom idle, held a bone needle and the rawhide sole for what would become a moccasin embroidered with a rainbow of porcupine quills.

"Did you come in a canoe over the water to be with the Akwanakai?" said the same little girl.

The little girl's older sister made a motion to shush her.

"Forgive my foolish sister, Oldest Grandmother! She is but five harvests and her questions mean no disrespect."

"Remember, Te Ata, that we learn by our questions. Come to me, littlest one." The old woman opened her arms and lifted the hesitant girl to her lap. "You are not disrespectful, child, but instead I am grateful to you for reminding me that all good song-stories must start from the beginning."

"Oldest Grandmother," an older boy spoke up, "all know that you have the wisdom of the great healer Sawahna. But did she not die before you came to us?"

"Oh, that is just part of the story. And perhaps that is the best place to start. Sawahna's care guided our people for many harvests long before even your mother or mother's mother was born.

"And in a sacred and mysterious way she was able to pass her skill and knowledge to me. For when Sawahna's time on our Mother Earth had passed and she was laid in the hill of our dead, her spirit went forward many, many harvests and entered an unborn child that was as yet without a spirit. Sawahna became the white Bear-Face child Becca. In the mystery that is The Great Spirit, Sawahna lived through another so that she could return and share her wisdom and aid her people."

The old woman smiled and kissed the head of the child nestled in her lap.

"That spirit was me. I know it is hard to understand. The song I sing to you tells how and why I returned to my true people, the Awkanakai."

She spread her arms wide to include the children who gathered before her.

"Spirit goes beyond time and place. But so you may understand, think of my strange journey as though putting beads upon a string. The first and most important bead is the spirit of love which may journey beyond what our eyes know.

"When I became the healer Chenoa and brought Sawahna's love back to my true people, here I found a Spirit Sister who was called Nemisa, the Singing Bird. She promised that when she left the land of Akwanakai, she would sing my song in a faraway time and place—in the world of the Bear-Faces.

The old woman's rheumy, dark eyes stared into the fire's flickering flames to a place and time far beyond the children and the circular wigwam walls.

"Cherish this song in your hearts. Sing it to your children and your children's children so that some far away day my Spirit Sister might hear the song and know the love I will always bear for her. She will know that her people never forgot her."

In a wavering voice she began, "Spirit Sister, I sing your song."

ONE

Gramma's back was turned, the faucet running. At the tinkling clatter of silverware against plates, I inched my hand across the table. My fingers closed over a warm butterscotch-oatmeal cookie, and I eased it towards me. I dropped the cookie into the medicine pouch I'd made from cloth scraps scavenged from Gramma's sewing basket. Large, uneven stitches of yellow yarn held three sides of the bag together. More yellow yarn served as both a drawstring and a way to tie the pouch to my belt. OK, so the medicine pouch wasn't particularly authentic, not much like the ones at the Field Museum. But, hey, Ben wouldn't know the difference, anyway.

One cookie down, three more to go. Squinting into a frown, I contemplated the now uneven grid of cooling cookies. *Well, it's sure I can't take the next one from the same row. A little more to the right, maybe?* After a glance at Gramma, I let my hand snake out again toward the cookies.

"Becca, seeing as you're taking a couple cookies, be sure to take some for Ben, too."

My hand froze midway to the cookie grid. *Now, how the heck did she know what I was doing?* Gramma had her back to me, didn't even glance up from washing the dishes. Dismissing the mystery with a shrug, I chose the three biggest cookies and deposited them in my pouch.

Of course, the cookies could hardly qualify now as honest-to-goodness plunder. Plunder has to be something you steal. That was the rule me and Ben had agreed to a few summers back when we first started playing Indians in the pines. Well, Ben didn't need to know Gramma simply gave me the cookies. But an Indian brave never lies— especially not to her warrior blood-brother. *Aw, Ben won't care how I got them. To him, a cookie's a cookie.*

Gramma raised her voice above the clatter of the baking sheets she was piling into the dishpan. "Ben's mother called while you was out to the barn. She don't want you playing back by the creek again today. Said Ben come home yesterday wet, covered with mud. Think she's afraid he'll take sick with asthma, like last summer when you was here visiting."

I rolled my eyes to the ceiling. *Poor Ben. If he so much as clears his throat Mrs. Boersma has him in bed, compresses on his chest, a thermometer in his mouth. Hardly a fate worthy of a warrior, even a mini one like Ben.*

"We're not going to the creek today." I hesitated and swallowed hard. "We're going to play...I mean hang out in the pines."

I gave a shiver and studied Gramma's back, wanting to tell her everything. *True, Wanaga swore me to secrecy but, after all, I'd already broken my vow by telling Ben.* I chewed my lip. *Breaking my word—that wasn't right—but I had to tell Ben. Wanaga's game is getting way too scary. But tell something that far-fetched to Gramma? I can just hear her reaction.* "Why, Becca! Whatever put such a strange notion in your head?" *Then she'll laugh. Grownups always do things like that to kids.* "A real Indian? With feathers and war-paint?" *I can imagine her chuckle growing louder. "And in our pine woods, yet?"* Hands on her hips, Gramma would shake her head. *"Child, you always was the darndest for letting your imagination run off with you."*

I gave a sigh. *OK, scratch telling Gramma. After all, what can you expect? Gramma is special but still only a grownup. Why, even yesterday, Ben only half-believed me.*

He had cocked his head, eying me with his silly lopsided grin, "Aw, come on, Becca! What do you take me for? A little kid that'll swallow anything?"

I raised my chin several notches. *Well, Ben, after today, you'll know this isn't just another story I made up.* After a glance toward Gramma, I grabbed another cookie from the table. This time she didn't notice my theft. Success! I pushed the chair away from the table slowly. Convinced I hadn't made a sound, I tiptoed toward the screen door.

"Becca."

I froze with my hand on the doorknob. *What an Indian warrior Gramma would've made!*

"Yeah, Gramma?"

"Got your glasses on?"

I fished the hated glasses from the pocket of my jeans and grunted. *Might as well resign myself,* I thought, *to being an Indian brave with glasses thick as the bottom of a Coke bottle. It's that or risk tripping over my own feet.*

Gramma dunked another cookie sheet in the water. "You mind now, Becca. Watch out for rattlesnakes in them pines."

"Sure, Gramma. No problem."

I let the door slam behind me and bounded down the stairs. *Rattlesnakes? Boy, that's nothing. Gramma, if you only knew about what else was in those pine woods—Old Wanaga with honest-to-goodness dead-people scalps hanging from his belt.*

7

I took a big bite of my plunder to bolster my courage. The butterscotch morsels were still warm and gooey, the way I liked them best. I crammed the rest of the cookie into my mouth and took off at a run across the new-mown grass, past the white barn, the old over-turned outhouse, past the clothesline, where sheets rippled and snapped in the June breeze.

My destination was the tall poplars bordering the pasture where, suspended from a branch of the tallest tree, was a swing. This was my place to ponder the world, make up stories, or just give myself over, eyes closed, to the swing's hypnotic rhythm. Didn't make a bad lookout spot, either. When I swung really high my toes could nearly touch the leaves' silvery undersides, and I had a robin's view of the countryside with its patchwork quilt of gold and green fields.

Here and there a farmhouse sprouted from a feathered tuft of trees. A truck, trailing a cloud of dust, rumbled down the gray ribbon of gravel road. I watched it pass the hill where my grandparent's church stood, rumble past their white frame house and far down the road toward Zietema's red barn. Once past Uncle Pete's farm, the gray ribbon of road unraveled to a thread, and the truck vanished into the velvety deep-green of the woods.

My eyes returned to the field of knee-high grass that was a border between Grampa's farm and the hill the church sat on. Ben's house was three farms the other side of the church crossroads, where paved blacktop crossed gravel road. I knew Ben wouldn't take the road but, instead, the path that wound through the church field. The best grasshoppers in all of Michigan were in that field. Last summer, me and Ben captured some there as big around as my thumb. So why walk on the road? I shaded my eyes against the sun. Still no sign of Ben.

Wanting to feel the wind on my bare toes, I kicked off my sneakers and gave myself over to the swing's rhythm.

Lean back, aim my toes for the sky. Touch those silvery leaves? Hey, someday I will. Just a little higher is all it would take. Bending sharply forward, legs kinked back, I closed my eyes for the backward plunge. On the return swoop, when I figured my toes had reached their highest point, I opened my eyes. This time the closest leaf was only an inch, maybe two, away. *Now, what if next time I touch that leaf with my toe and the leaf falls to the ground? And what if it turns out to be, not a leaf at all, but instead the silver key to a magic kingdom? I'll pick it up and...I choked on the thought. No! Thoughts like those—wasn't that how, a week ago, Wanaga appeared?* I didn't want to risk any more make-believe crossing the line into reality. After all, the shell necklace with the rawhide cord had started out as make-believe, too. But then I had found the real thing buried under the pine needles.

Dragging my toes in the dirt, I stopped the swing. I was feeling that familiar, uneasy flutter in my stomach again. There's no reason to fear Wanaga, I told myself. I pictured his face, the smile that wrinkled his brown cheeks to crepe paper and folded his black eyes into slits. Squatting under a pine tree, he had told me the ancient stories of his people, his voice a purr of strange words. While he spoke, his gnarled brown fingers had whittled deadwood pine scraps into tiny detailed forms—a fox, a bear, a squirrel. If I came today he'd promised me he would carve the image of a raven, his own spirit form. The carving was to be his gift, an amulet he had called it, to put in my medicine pouch. This was the Wanaga I knew by day.

But at night? My heart began to pound as I thought of the nightmares I'd been having. They were so real and always the same. An Indian woman, long braids of black hair framing her dark face, her eyes sad, held out her arms like she was calling me. It didn't make sense, but I wanted to go to this strange, sad woman and let her wrap her arms around me. But then Wanaga would appear and beckon me in the opposite direction. When I turned toward him, the kindly old man of daylight changed. His smile was a cruel grimace and his eyes shrank to glowing black beads. A misty image of a raven took the place of the old man's body, until Wanaga, the man, was no more. The raven fixed his glittering unblinking gaze on me. I couldn't tear my eyes from its sharp, hooked beak and when I finally did I saw his curving talons. I tried to scream, but I couldn't make a sound. Somehow I knew the raven meant to gouge out my eyes, rip my flesh. I turned to run, wildly seeking that dark–faced kindly woman, but she had vanished. My legs were stumps, my arms frozen to my sides. I was alone with no way to stop the raven's attack.

I shuddered, remembering the dream. A nightmare, that's all it was. Dreams were weird. But then what could be more weird than Wanaga. Sometimes I thought maybe I was going crazy. That was part of the reason I wanted to take Ben with me today. If he saw Wanaga too, then I wasn't crazy. Though I'm not sure that being crazy might be better than Wanaga being a reality. Even though in movies and TV the Indians were always the villains, I'd never felt that way. It made me sad to see how their land was stolen and sometimes it even made me cry when I watched the soldiers or settlers kill them on TV. *Funny how when I was a little kid I had good dreams of a kindly old woman, her face brown, her eyes black and her long thin braids silver. I was crying for my mother in the dream, and the old woman enfolded me in her arms. She sang a song in soft flowing words I did not understand but the sound comforted me, and I knew I need not be afraid. She would care for me. I needed that dream to replace the nightmare of Wanaga. I shook my head to clear my mind of dreams. Enough with dreams already! Get with reality, girl!*

I scanned the field for Ben. Still no sign of him. *What if Mrs. Boersma won't let him come? If Ben doesn't show up today I won't go to the pines either. After all, there are plenty of other things to do. Grampa said the old mother cat has a new litter of kittens hidden somewhere up in the barn loft. Or I can go to Uncle Pete's woods and finish the bridge of deadwood me and Ben are building across the creek. Or I could catch some more grasshoppers.* I'd been keeping a collection of live ones in a canning jar stuffed with grass and stored under my bed. *Anything but face Wanaga alone.*

Two small figures sauntering across the churchyard caught my eye. The two entered the field, single file, following the narrow twisting path through the long grass. As they drew closer, I pushed my glasses further up on my nose and squinted into the field. *Yes, that's Ben all right, with his spiky blond hair and always sunburned face. But who's that with him?*

My face fell as I squinted toward the blurred figure and saw it slowly focus into a girl, taller than Ben, her hair long and blonde. A knot rose in my throat. *How could Ben betray our secret? And to of all people Charlene Boersma!*

Charlene, Ben's older sister by about three years had always been the girl Mama, even Gramma, proclaimed the perfect friend for me. Their reasoning? Charlene was a girl my age and always the "little lady," a label Gramma favored and I considered pathetic. Charlene never saw the people in our imaginary games or lived the adventure the way me and Ben did. Any game remotely exciting or adventurous always ended on Charlene's favorite sour note. Her nose in the air, she'd say, "Boy, this is really dumb. What are you, Becca, ten years old? I'm going home."

OK, maybe I was a little old to be playing make-believe, but I wanted to enjoy one last summer of pretend.

Honestly, I dreaded eighth grade. Seventh grade had been a disaster. I was a head taller than all the boys, so forget junior high dances where I desperately tried to look "cool" while other girls got asked to dance. And sports?

Well, when I saw a ball coming at me, my first thought was to duck, not catch it. I was happiest reading a book or writing down the stories in my head, so I guess I was the class nerd.

I fought the impulse to run into the house as I watched the two approaching. Head down, Ben was shuffling dejectedly behind Charlene. Appropriate enough behavior for a traitor, I thought. But then maybe he had no choice. Even a brave warrior can buckle under torture. I vowed to keep that in mind, until I knew the facts.

At the opening in the barbed-wire fence that separated Grampa's yard from the church field, Charlene paused to carefully check her clothing. Wrinkling her nose with disgust, she brushed a bug from her pink shorts, then pulled a field burr from her sock.

Spotting me, she called out in a bored voice, "Oh, hi, Becca."

Ben peered around his sister's shoulder, managed a limp wave, then ducked back into Charlene's shadow. Undaunted by my non-existent greeting, Charlene started up the grassy slope that led to the poplars and my swing. I watched her curls bounce, glowing gold in the sunlight and gave one of my own thin brown braids a disdainful toss over my shoulder. I sighed. OK, so Charlene was everything girls were supposed to be. "Petite"—girls like Charlene were never short. She had a pretty doll face with blue eyes, and her clothes never showed a speck of dirt. She made me feel like a skinny, ungainly daddy longlegs perched beside a butterfly.

Charlene, smirking, stopped a few feet from my swing and crossed her arms over her chest. "My mom wouldn't let Ben come unless I came along too."

I searched Ben's eyes. He gave a helpless shrug.

With an offhand toss of her head in Ben's direction, Charlene said, "He was sick with a cold most of last week. Yesterday was the first day Mom let him out to play. And, boy, was she ever mad that you two were playing in the creek again. Ben takes sick awful easy, you know."

"Aw, jeez, ain't nothing wrong with me," Ben said.

Charlene ignored him. "Anyways, my mom says I'm to see he don't fall in the creek again."

Being stuck with Charlene for a day was a problem, but I figured I had to make the effort to put up with her, for Ben's sake. Maybe we'd explore the barn loft, an activity that was off limits and therefore worthy of consideration. (On second thought, not for Charlene. I could just hear her, "Ick, it's too dirty and probably full of mice!") We could go back to Gramma's and play Clue or Monopoly. But what really worried me was how much Ben had told Charlene about Wanaga. I hoped nothing.

Charlene gave a bored yawn. "So, Becca, when'd you get here?"

"About a week ago," I mumbled.

"Her mother's staying with their new baby, so Becca come all by herself this time on the train," Ben said, admiration in his voice. "And all the way from Chicago... at night, too."

Charlene slowly twisted a strand of hair around her finger. "So? Big deal. Pamela Overweg went all the way to California on a train last summer, and she was only ten." Charlene gave my dirty feet the same look she would have given a long-dead mouse. "Hey, don't you know, Becca, you can get terrible diseases from going barefoot? Worms...lockjaw."

"Who said?" I muttered.

"I just know," Charlene said, with a toss of her head. "And lockjaw will kill you dead, too."

"Aw, that's stupid!" I looked longingly toward the house, wishing I had followed my first instinct and run inside at the first sight of Charlene. Too late now. I made what I hoped was a casual grab for my sneakers, but carefully checked the bottom of my feet for worms before I put the first shoe on. I avoided Charlene's face, not wanting to see the smirk I knew would be there. "OK," I said, sighing with resignation, "so, what do you guys want to do?"

Charlene choked on a giggle. "Why, Becca, what do you mean, what do we want to do? Ben said you were going to show him this real Indian of yours." She drew out the word "real" in a syrupy singsong. "Supposed to live in your grandpa's pines. Wears war paint and feathers, so I hear."

Charlene's words hit me like a slap in the face. I glared at Ben, and said, "How could you tell her? We both took an oath of secrecy!"

"Oh, give me a break!" Charlene groaned. "Becca, are you almost thirteen…or more like going on ten, like Ben?"

Ben swallowed hard and swiped at the tear trickling down his cheek. His voice came out in a hoarse stutter. "Mom wouldn't let me come without her, and…and, well, Charlene said she wasn't gonna go with me. I… I thought if I told her about Wanaga, maybe then she would come." He gave a loud sniff. "I'm sorry. Honest, Becca."

I drew in a deep breath. OK, I thought, so what right have I got being mad at Ben? Didn't I break my own oath to Wanaga when I told Ben? I returned Charlene's cat grin with an icy stare.

Charlene gave her curls a self-righteous toss. "You know, you got Ben really believing there's an Indian living in those pines. Talk about stupid! Why those pines aren't even a woods. Bet you didn't know that. They're only a windbreak your grandpa planted a long time ago. Ever notice how the pine trees grow in even rows, like a field of corn? Don't it seem a little strange a 'wild' Indian would want to live in some farmer's windbreak?"

"OK, so it's strange," I said. "But there **is** an Indian in those pines." I met Charlene's eyes and stared her down.

"And I'll show him to you, too!" I rather relished the idea that she might become as scared of Wanaga as I was.

I bolted from the swing and set out at a fast trot for Grampa's back pasture bordering the pines. Feeling Ben slip his hand into mine, I looked down into his freckled, sunburned face and my prickling anger faded.

"Hey, we're gonna show her, huh, Becca?"

I gave a limp nod. "Yeah, sure are." I hoped my voice sounded more confident than I felt. I was afraid Wanaga would be angry that I had dared to bring Charlene and Ben to the pines. Maybe he would never want to appear to me again, but then that might be all for the best. The humiliation Charlene would inflict on me might just be worth it if the nightmares stopped.

"Hey, you guys, wait," Charlene called.

I paused at the chicken coop and let her catch up.

"Hey, Becca, what do you and your Indian do out there?" Charlene asked, gasping for breath.

"He tells her stories," Ben said when I said nothing.

Charlene giggled. "About what? Cowboys and Indians?"

I stopped abruptly and spun on my heels to face Charlene. "Don't you know anything? There were no cowboys around here."

"Oh, I know that, but I'm not so sure you do. So this Wa...Wanug...well, whatever his name, he tells you stories?"

Ben raised his voice, hoping to help. "He tells her stories about the first Indian that ever lived. His name was Grandfather and he was sitting in this canoe all alone, because it was before the earth was made. Then there was this woodchuck who come up from the water and brought him this big glob of—"

I cut him off. "Ben, just hush, would you?"

Charlene sputtered out a laugh. "Aw, come on, Becca, it was just getting good."

I shot a glance at Ben that clearly said, "Don't say any more."

"This Indian of yours," Charlene continued, "speaks English, does he?"

"No."

"Then how can you understand him?"

"I don't know. He just talks. I hear a strange language, but somehow in my brain I know what he's saying."

"Sure, Becca. You believe in the Easter Bunny, too?"

I walked faster.

"Is what's-his-name a Michigan Indian?"

I dropped to my belly, wiggled under the barbed wire fence, then sprang to my feet to help pull Ben through. "Yeah, Charlene, matter of fact, he is a Michigan Indian."

Eyeing our t-shirts with disgust, Charlene wrinkled her nose. "Just look at you two. You're both filthy." She crossed her arms over her chest and stuck her nose in the air. "You can bet I'm not crawling under that fence."

I gave a shrug and started toward the pines, Ben at my heels. I called over my shoulder, "So, suit yourself. See if we care. Oh, Charlene, there's a gate at the far end of the pasture. Of course you'll have to wade through the wild blackberry thorns. A thick patch of them, too. Have fun!"

"Hey, wait you guys. I can't...."

Ben and I walked faster but, by the time we'd reached the middle of the pasture, Charlene had caught up to us again. I noted with satisfaction that the front of her t-shirt was as dirty as my own.

She cleared her throat importantly. "Hey, Becca, just what tribe is this Indian of yours supposed to be from?"

"Akwanakai."

Charlene gave a gleeful snort. "Hah! Now, that just shows you made up this whole thing. In school last year we had to learn about our state's history. The Potawatomi and Huron were the tribes that lived near this part of Michigan, and they haven't lived here for a hundred and fifty years. See, Ben. She doesn't know what she's talking about."

I clenched my teeth, keeping my eyes straight ahead. "You'll see, Charlene. He's real!"

"OK, if he's so real, Becca, then how come he doesn't wear regular clothes? Don't you know real Indians don't dress up anymore in feathers and war paint?"

Ben spoke up. "Well, this one does. And you know what else, Charlene? Wanaga even has scalps hanging on his belt."

I winced. *Oh, Ben just shut up!*

"Oh, wow!" Charlene said between giggles. "This keeps getting better and better."

I fought the anger and, with some effort, kept my voice steady. "Wanaga sometimes lives in Grampa's pines, but he isn't from our time. He came from long ago."

Charlene snorted. "So, now there's a ghost in your grandpa's pines?"

"No, Wanaga's as alive as you are."

"Well, then, how come he can't even remember what tribe he came from?"

"He does, and it's not Potawatomi! Look, Charlene Boersma, you don't know everything."

"Maybe I don't, but it's for sure I know a lot more about Indians than you."

Minutes later we stood in the small pine clearing where Wanaga had first appeared to me. Slowly my eyes adjusted to the dark, for the only light came from the droplets of sunlight that filtered through the thick pine branches.

"Go ahead, Becca," Ben said, squeezing my hand. "Show Charlene the necklace."

My heart was a pounding drum in my chest as I walked toward the tallest pine, knelt and dug my hand deep into the rust-colored carpet of pine needles. My fingers touched something smooth and hard. Pulling out the necklace, I carefully unwound the rawhide cord from the pendant. I brushed my fingers over the shell pendant suspended from a band of brilliant red, blue, and yellow embroidered porcupine quills. My hands shook as I placed the rawhide cord over my head. The pendant rested heavily on my chest. Through my t-shirt, I felt the shell's strange warmth, as if it was alive.

Charlene and Ben pressed close.

"See, Charlene," Ben said, "didn't I tell you? She really has a honest-to-goodness Indian necklace."

"Aw, she could've bought it at that dime store in Zeeland—that one that sells tourist stuff."

But she kept inching closer, reaching out to touch the pendant. "What's that scratched onto the shell?" she asked. "It's so dark in here, it's hard to see."

"A panther."

Charlene tried to laugh but it came out instead as a nervous sputter. "It's for sure, then, that necklace isn't Indian. Panthers are from Africa. Everybody knows that."

"Wanaga said that a long time ago giant wildcats lived in this forest and the Akwanakai called them panthers."

Charlene gave a shrug. "Oh, yeah, pretty sure! I suppose next you'll tell me elephants lived here, too?"

Ben pulled on my arm to get my attention. "Becca, why don't you make Wanaga come…now? That'll show her!"

I drew in a deep breath. "OK, but you two gotta stay over there. I don't know if I can do it, if you're both crowding me."

Ben solemnly nodded. Charlene sat back, muttering, "Oh, brother, what next?"

I knelt upon the same spot where I had dug up the necklace, tipped my head back and raised my arms toward the clearing's pine-branch roof. Taking a deep breath, I began the chant Wanaga had taught me, my mind struggling to bring the strange sounds to my lips. I hesitated, floundering desperately for the next word.

"Becca," Charlene said, her voice shaky, "this is getting too weird. I don't want to do this anymore."

I fought to keep Charlene's voice distant. In my mind, I managed to summon Wanaga's words, "Go deep, Becca. Deep inside. Feel the magic, the power. Deep, deep within. Come to me." I heard a voice raised in an eerie trill of strange words. A being inside me, yet somehow apart, had once again taken over the song from me.

"A raven. There it is," Ben shouted, pointing to a high branch. "It's Wanaga!"

At Ben's cry, the being that sang through me vanished, and I looked up with a start.

"Oh, big deal," Charlene said, her voice a little too loud. "Just some big old crow sitting on a pine branch. So, that's your Indian, Becca?"

I stared up at the glossy black raven and lowered my voice to a pleading whisper. "Wanaga, come to me. I open myself to your power."

Charlene's eyes went big with fear. Her voice trembled on the verge of tears. "Becca, stop it! This is too spooky. It's like you're calling the devil or something!"

I extended my arms toward the raven. "Wanaga, show yourself. Please, don't be angry. I didn't mean to tell them."

The crow screamed, its call a raucous laugh. It lifted its wings and disappeared through an opening in the pine-branch roof.

Slowly, I stood. Drawing in a deep breath, I faced Charlene and Ben, who were both cowering on the opposite side of the clearing. "Guess Wanaga is angry that you know about him. He won't come."

Charlene drew herself up straight and made a grab for Ben's hand. She started to talk, but her voice came out in a nervous squeak. She cleared her throat and tried again.

"That was only a crow up in that tree, and you know it. You just wait until I tell my mom about what you've been doing in these pines. Devil stuff! She'll never let Ben play with you again. You're crazy, Becca Morrison! A real loony!"

She stomped out of the clearing, dragging a sniffling Ben behind her.

I sank to the pine needles and buried my head in my hands. I had lost Ben and Wanaga both. Hearing the soft rustle of pine needles, I raised my head slightly, thinking maybe Ben had returned. Through the blur of tears, I saw first his moccasins, then the fringe of his leggings, and the porcupine embroidery on the garter he always tied around his leg. But what drew my gaze relentlessly were the scalps. A cold shiver went through me. Wanaga had come.

TWO

The clearing was strangely silent. No birds sang. Even the breeze that had been softly whining through the pine branches had stilled. I felt the cold prickle of fear.

No, I won't be afraid. I won't!

I slowly raised my head. My eyes lit on the scalp locks, five long tails of coarse black hair, each dangling from his belt like a thick clump of fringe.

I swallowed hard. *OK, so he had killed some people, but he had an excuse.* Wanaga had explained that those scalps had been from Iroquois warriors who would have killed him with their war clubs if he hadn't done them in first. *Fair enough, and, yet, to wear a dead man's hair as decoration and give it no more thought than Daddy might give a necktie?* I shuddered.

Wanaga was bare chested, his dark tan skin painted with horizontal, jagged lines of black, red, and yellow. Around his neck he wore a circular necklace of bear claws, each giant, curving claw separated from the next by a small blue shell.

I looked at his face and gasped. His eyes! Black, glowing, they belonged to the Wanaga of my nightmares. Blindly, I scrambled backward, falling into the dead, rust-colored branches. The pine's bone-dry fingers snatched at my hair and clothes, lashed out at my face and arms. My back against the trunk, trapped, I watched Wanaga slowly advance.

He stopped a foot from where I cowered. His lips curled into a snarl. In his own language, his voice boomed, "You betrayed me! Never again will I trust you. The necklace. Give it to me!"

Frozen with fear, I could only stare mutely at him.

He fixed his black raven eyes on me. "You understand the tongue of the Akwanakai. Do not pretend it otherwise. Day after day, I have opened your ears to my words. Hear me now. You will obey! The necklace!"

I burrowed deeper into the branches. My eyes darted around him to the opposite side of the clearing where the tangle of pine trees opened onto the path that led back to the sunlit pasture. Wanaga's arm whipped out toward me. I ducked, burying my head in my arms to fend off the blow. But he didn't hit me. Instead, I felt his fingers close around the shell pendant of the necklace. Hearing Wanaga scream, I looked up and saw the old man's face contorted with pain. He was massaging his hand as though it'd been burned.

Seeing a chance to escape, I darted out from the entangling bushes on hands and knees and scurried around the old man's legs. I jumped to my feet and ran for the path. Too late, I saw him. Legs spread, arms crossed over his chest, Wanaga stood blocking the path. I slammed into him. He grabbed my wrist, his curved, yellow fingernails digging into my flesh.

He glowered down at me. "So, Little Mouse, you think to leave me?"

My voice trembled. "But you were over there just a second ago. How did you get—" My words choked in a gulp of fear.

He gave a hissing laugh. "I have great powers. Time...moving—they are as nothing to me. And now,

Little Mouse, my necklace. Return it to me." His raven eyes focused greedily on the shell pendant.

I remembered his scream of pain when he had tried to pull it from my neck. Some strange magic, I thought, must make this necklace hot to the touch of anyone but its wearer. He won't try to take it from me again. At least I hope not. I fought to steady my voice. "I...I'll give you your necklace, but only if you'll let me go home. Now. Right now."

He released my arm, but his eyes remained fixed on the pendant, as sweat beaded on his forehead. I took several steps backward.

Anxiously, he licked his lips, then extended his hand, palm up, toward me. "I released you. The necklace. Put it in my hand."

Now is the time to put my imagination to good use. I'll pretend I'm courageous. I raised my chin and drew back my shoulders. "No, Wanaga, not until I'm out of here will you get this necklace. I'll toss it to you from the pasture fence. And then I'm never coming back to these pines. Not ever!"

Wanaga tensed, as though my words had been a blow. His beady, glowing eyes became the filmy eyes of an old man. His features, no longer twisted in rage, didn't seem as sharp, as scary. He stood before me, shoulders stooped, his expression one of sorrow. "Becca, do not turn from me now. I journeyed so far to find you." Tears trickled down the deep furrows in his cheeks.

My head ached with confusion. *Is what just happened part of a nightmare? This sad old man who's standing in front of me seems so harmless, but only a minute ago....* I looked down at my t-shirt. The necklace was still there. My arms bore the red scratches of the pine branches, my wrists the half-moon marks of his fingernails. *It has to be real.*

"No, I want to go home," I said, my voice shaking. "And I still won't give you your necklace until—"

"But, Becca, the necklace is my gift to you."

"B…but, you said…."

"Becca, you are so frightened. Why?"

"You know darned well why! Don't you remember how you—"

"Ah, forgive an old man. But I only feared for your safety if you were to take the necklace… well, too soon. There is great medicine in it, Becca. 'Power' in the language of your people. Evil, even death, might befall one who is ignorant of its medicine."

I enclosed the shell pendant in my fingers and felt its strange warmth. Looking toward the old man, I wondered if I dared trust him again. No, I decided. I've had enough of Wanaga's magic. "I don't want your necklace," I told him. "I just want to go home and never come back here."

He stepped to one side, freeing the path. "Becca, never would I hold you against your will. You are free to go."

I walked warily toward the path, ready to bolt if he made a grab for me.

Instead, he sank to his haunches and buried his head in his hands. "If only I could have reached you with my words, made you understand," he mumbled through his hands.

I hurried past him. At the sound of a muffled sob, I turned. His shoulders were heaving. Wondering whether his sorrow was genuine, I hesitated, then said, "Wanaga, don't worry about the necklace. I promise I'll leave it where I said I would. Honest, I will." He did not respond. "Wanaga, are you OK?"

"Forgive a foolish old man his tears. I cry not for myself but for one who is very important to me, a woman of the Akwanakai. You, Becca, were my only hope to free her."

"Me?"

"Ah, but now you leave, never to return." He gave another loud sob.

I looked toward the distant shafts of sunlight where the path opened onto the pasture, then back to Wanaga huddled forlornly on the ground.

"But, Wanaga, I'm just a kid. Why do you think I can help?"

He raised his head, his eyes seeking me out in the shadows. "I sensed in your spirit, Becca, a kinship to the Akwanakai. That is why, to your eyes alone, have I appeared as a man. This... this Ben and Charlene," he said, spitting out their names like something bitter in his mouth, "and, indeed, any of your people, shall see only Wanaga the raven. Ah, but now, Becca, you are to leave me forever." He hid his face again in his hands. "All is lost." He peered up at me through the web of his fingers.

Anxiously, I looked back toward the path, then toward Wanaga. "Well, maybe, I could help you after all. I mean, I still want to go home, you understand. And...and, I'm still going to keep this necklace, until I get as far as the pasture fence. That's not going to change." I thought that a wise precaution to add, just in case. "But...well, if I can help you, I'll try."

He looked up, a broad smile beginning to crinkle his face. "My Little One, you return joy to an old man's heart."

I began to wonder if Wanaga hadn't recovered from his sorrow a bit too quickly.

He stood and held his hand out to me. I shook my head and retreated another step.

"Ah, Becca, I see you still do not trust me. Very well, follow me then."

"But where are we going?"

"To the hill where your people have built a giant white wigwam with a roof that points sharp as a spear to the sky. Upon the spear, two saplings are bound together like this." He held his arms in the form of a cross.

"But, Wanaga, that's the church. Why do you want to go there?"

"Soon, Becca...soon you will understand."

Wanaga parted the branches and began to wind his way among the rows of pines toward the church. I followed him, careful to keep a safe distance of several steps. He stopped where the pines opened onto the churchyard and motioned for me to stand at his side. I shook my head. No way was I going that close to him!

"But, Becca, from where you stand within the trees, you cannot see."

I peeked around a branch and squinted into the bright sunlight. The white church with its tall spire and arching stained-glass window sat upon the softly sloping hill of just-mown grass. I knew that the minister's house, though now hidden from sight behind the church, was close, only across the road. Reverend Holstege had a big family. *Someone is bound to be home. In fact, maybe his kids are playing in the front yard. If Wanaga tries to grab me, I'll just run screaming for their house.* Squaring my shoulders, I stepped into the bright sunlight and walked toward where he stood, a frown on his face, contemplating the church grounds.

With a sweeping gesture of his arms, he took in the church, its yard, the pines behind him. "All this you see, Becca, from horizon to horizon, was once the land of my people, the Akwanakai. Mighty trees, the grandfathers of those your people now call oak, maple, and elm, they grew in great forests that extended as far as the eye could see. The deer, the bear, all animals, even the mighty panther, they lived in the forests, and we called them brothers." His face darkened. "But, now, the Akwanakai, the great forests, the animals, all are gone." He spit onto the ground. "All destroyed by your people."

I swallowed hard. "I know how bad you must feel, Wanaga. And I'm awful sorry, but that was a long time ago. Nobody's even alive anymore who had anything to do with what happened to the forests and your people."

"Ah, Becca, my Little One, have no fear. I do not come for revenge."

"Then why?"

"This mound of earth, where now stands this giant wigwam of your people, is a sacred place of the Akwanakai. Watch carefully, Becca, that you may understand, and perhaps...." He narrowed his eyes as he pondered my face. "Yes, and perhaps, it may be that my Little One may remember."

"But—"

"Hush, now. I must have silence."

He knelt and took from the medicine pouch hanging on his belt a gray pebble, a withered bird's foot, and a small buckskin bag. Loosening the bag's drawstrings, he poured into his palm a red powder. He spit on it, then with his thumb mixed powder and saliva to a red sticky paste. I watched as he smeared the paste in a jagged line from the bridge of his nose to each ear.

He turned to me. "Now, I paint your face."

I drew back from him. After seeing him spit in the powder, I wasn't going to wear that on my face. "No!" I said, my voice louder than I had wanted. His face fell, as though he was greatly offended.

"Wanaga, I don't want to hurt your feelings or anything it's just...I...." I gave a sigh. "Oh, OK, you can paint my face."

I wrinkled my nose as I felt his finger smear the paint across my cheeks. *OK, so wearing an old man's spit on my face is disgusting, but at least it's better than getting worms from going barefoot.*

Wanaga stepped back to check out my face and nodded, apparently pleased with his handiwork. Handing me the gray pebble, he told me to hold it in my right hand. The bird's foot he kept for himself. He knelt and began to chant, his voice a soft, eerie mumble of strange sounds. From the direction of the churchyard, I heard other voices that seemed to join in his chant. The voices, though, were muffled as though carried on the wind and coming from far away. Hearing the slow throb of a drum, I turned toward the sound. A mist now covered the hill, so thick I couldn't even see the church.

Wanaga stood and stretched an arm toward the hill. "Behold the Sacred Hill of the Akwanakai."

The mist receded, as though answering Wanaga's command. Gone now was the church. The hill was still there but was covered all over with small piles of what looked like clay pots, bows, quivers of arrows, and things I couldn't even name.

Wanaga pointed toward the far side of the hill. "See. They come."

The chanting and drumbeats grew louder. Fear knotted my stomach as I watched a string of misty figures come into focus and begin to climb the hill. At the front of the procession two men, dressed only in breechcloths, carried on their shoulders a long piece of wood, and on it was a long narrow bundle wrapped in what looked like an animal skin. Behind them men and women plodded slowly up the hill, their feet seeming to keep time with the drum beat. Here and there, a naked child held onto a woman's skirt. As they came closer, I could see their faces. All, even the children's, were painted black as coal and striped with red.

This was getting way too weird. I looked toward Wanaga, pleading, "Shouldn't we hide in the pines? What if they see us?"

"They cannot see us, for we exist only in the time of your people. My medicine removed from your eyes the cloud that has kept you from looking into the past."

I shook my head. "I don't understand any of this. I'm scared, Wanaga. I just want to go home."

"Soon, Little One, soon." He pointed toward the hill. "See. They lay her now in her grave."

The procession had stopped at the top of the hill. I watched the men gently lay the platform on the grass. A loud, eerie wail went up from the crowd as the men lifted the fur-wrapped bundle from the slab of wood, tied it with cords, and lowered it slowly into the ground.

Shivering, I wrapped my arms around my chest. "It's getting so cold, Wanaga. Please, I'm afraid." I sank to the ground. It suddenly became dark. I felt like a heavy weight was pressing down on my chest. I couldn't breathe. "Wanaga!" I screamed. "Wanaga!"

* * *

"Wake, Little One. You're dreaming. Of course you can breathe."

I gasped and looked around. I was back in the pine clearing. Wanaga was squatting at my side, his arm around my shoulder.

I shook off his arm and stood. "How'd I get back here?"

"I brought you here when you fainted."

"Then I didn't dream about you taking me to the church hill…or did I?"

He shook his head.

"Wanaga, I don't ever want to go there again."

"Little One, I'm sorry you were afraid, but there was no other way for you to understand the reason I have come."

"But I don't understand. Not at all!"

"That hill contains the bones of my people, the gifts given to their spirits so that they might possess all they needed for their journey to the land of the dead. Your people showed dishonor to this sacred place, dug deep into the hill and removed the bones, the gifts, belonging to the woman, Sawahna, whose body you saw lowered into her grave. She was a great medicine woman of the Akwanakai. But Sawahna was far more to me."

He stared into the forest shadows, seeing a vision I could not. "As children we both had powers beyond our years. At the feet of a great Akwanakai holy man we sat together as though brother and sister learning the sacred medicine of the Spirit World."

"And Sawahna's the woman you came to free?"

He nodded.

"But that can't be. She's dead. I watched them bury her."

"Ah, no, Little One, she exists somewhere between life and death. Tormented, her spirit wanders in and out of time, unable to find peace. And that is why I came to seek you out."

"Me?"

"Long ago, your blood-kin stole Sawahna's bones and her spirit gifts. They hid them away in their wigwam. Only when the bones and the gifts are returned to their rightful place under the earth of the Hill of the Dead will Sawahna find peace."

"But my grandma and grandpa don't have anybody's bones. They don't know anything about that hill, except that their church is built there."

"Becca, you must help me. Help Sawahna. Your people, they have stolen from the Akwanakai so much that can never be returned—the forest, the animals, the land. Sawahna's bones, they alone can be returned. And, you, Becca, can do this."

"But—"

"Please, Becca, help us." His black, squinty eyes bored into me.

My voice quivered. "All right, I'll try and find out something." I walked toward the path, then turned to face Wanaga. He seemed such a forlorn old man now, hardly someone to fear. I took the necklace from my neck and held it out to him. "Here's your necklace back."

He laughed, his voice a harsh cackle like the call of a crow. "Ah, then, Little Mouse, you no longer fear me? I am glad. I will leave the necklace here for you. You will need it to summon me, once you have found Sawahna's bones. "

I turned and ran without stopping until I reached the sunny pasture where I felt like I could breathe again.

THREE

Early next morning, I sat on the edge of Gramma's bed watching her dress for church. She was wearing a silky, navy-blue dress with white polka dots, the one she wore every Sunday. Short and round, Gramma was way over sixty, though her hair was still brown, with only a gray strand here and there. She picked up a small blue hat, a white flower in its brim, and carefully centered it on her head. Catching my down-in-the-dumps expression, she flashed me a smile.

"My, aren't you the sad sack this morning."

I shrugged.

Gramma walked to the bed and felt my forehead. "You feeling poorly?"

I shook my head. The thought had crossed my mind to fake being sick, but I was determined to go to church and see that the building was still there, to make sure nothing had changed. And going with Gramma and Grampa, that was safe. Never again would I go to the church hill alone—for sure not with Wanaga.

"Maybe you're just homesick for Mama and Daddy, huh?"

"Oh, no. I'm OK," I said. "It's just...." I tried to find something safe to say. "Guess it's just this dress. I hate the stiff lace on the collar. Always makes my neck itch."

Gramma sank down on the bed and enclosed me in a hug. "Well, you do look awful pretty in it, anyways. And I know what you mean about Sunday clothes. I dare say I'd much rather have on my old blueberry-picking overalls than this girdle and fancy dress. Now, wouldn't we make tongues wag if we was to show up in church, you in your blue jeans and me in my old raggedy overalls?"

I couldn't help a laugh and threw my arms around Gramma. "I love you, Gramma!" Clinging to the soft cushion that was Gramma, breathing in her Sunday smell of rosewater cologne and peppermint candy, I could almost forget Wanaga.

"Anna...ANNA," Grampa called from the opposite end of the house.

"In the bedroom, Papa," Gramma called back.

Grampa's name was Peter but, as far as I knew, no one ever called him that. Gramma, my mother, aunts, uncles, they all called him Papa. And people outside the family just called him Doc. He had been a father and Zeeland's veterinarian for so many years, I figured people must have long forgotten Grampa's real name. How awful to lose your name like that. But, well, Grampa didn't seem to mind.

He appeared at the bedroom door, his tall, stoop-shouldered frame filling the doorway. His hair was thick, slivery-white, like silky milkweed strands when they were ready to burst from their pod.

"Anna...can't find my pipe anywheres."

"On the end table by the piano."

Grampa turned to go. "Wait, Papa, your tie's on crooked."

Grampa was the only person I knew who wore a bowtie and always the same red plaid one, every Sunday.

Patiently, he stood in the doorway like an oversized little boy while Gramma straightened his tie.

She turned to me. "Now go get your pink sash that goes with your dress."

As soon as Gramma's back was turned, I rolled my eyes. The pink dress and sash, all ruffles and poufy gathered skirt had been a birthday gift from Aunt Sophie. There was no way Mama was about to let me exchange it for a dress I would wear instead of something for a ten-year-old.

I retrieved the crumpled sash from the corner of my bureau drawer, where I had wadded it into a tight ball after church the week before, clomped downstairs and glumly handed it to Gramma.

Shaking her head, Gramma tried to smooth the wrinkles. "Well, 'leastways you didn't lose it. Can't say that does much for the way it looks though." She glanced at the noisily ticking alarm clock on her nightstand. "No time left to set up the ironing board. Guess we'll have to make do."

Gramma gave me the once over and frowned. "Becca, you got pine needles stuck in your hair. I'm sorry, child, but you can't go to church looking like a porcupine. Ain't civilized."

I retreated to the bathroom where I tugged out the majority of the offending pine needles, gritting my teeth the whole time. Then I returned to Gramma's bedroom for final inspection. This time I passed.

I sat beside Gramma on the bed while she hunted through her pocketbook to make sure she had her church offering.

"Gramma?"

"Yes, Becca?" she mumbled, preoccupied.

"Do you think that real Indians used to live around here once?"

"Now, what did I do with the church envelope? I thought sure I put it in in my pocketbook last night. Ah, here it is." She fished out a small blue envelope.

"But, Gramma, the Indians?"

"Indians?"

"Yeah, the ones who used to live around here."

"Oh, no doubt some lived around here, but a very long time ago. Why, even when your great-grandma and grandpa come over here from Holland the Indians was long gone. Though I heard tell that—"

"Anna," Grampa called from the living room. "Can't find my suit coat."

"What did you hear, Gramma?"

"Oh, later, Becca. I got to help Grampa find his coat or, sure as the world, we'll be late again for church."

"Anna...ANNA!"

"I'm coming, Papa."

Minutes later I was walking between Gramma and Grampa on the gravel road that led to the church. Careful to keep my eyes from the hill, I concentrated on the little puffs of dust that rose as I scuffed each foot in the gravel.

Glancing toward Gramma, I tried again. "Do you think that Indians once walked where we're walking right now?"

"Well, I don't know that they...." Gramma glanced down at my feet. "Becca Morrison, just look what you're doing to your Sunday shoes. Now they're covered with dust."

Grampa took my hand and gave it a gentle squeeze. "Becca, I wouldn't doubt a minute that Indians walked on this very same spot. Why, when your Uncle Frank was growing up he used to find arrowheads in the fresh-plowed fields all the time."

"What tribe lived around here, Grampa?"

"Oh, I think it must have been Huron or Potawatomi."

My face fell. "Sure it wasn't a tribe called Akwanakai?"

Grampa thought a moment, then shook his head. "Can't say I ever heard of them. No, it was Potawatomi, and maybe a few Huron, lived in this part of Michigan. I'm pretty sure of that. Hey, Anna, whatever happened to that box of bones, pottery chips, and whatnot? You know, all that stuff they found when the church foundation was being dug?"

"Don't Jenny have it all?"

"Remember, Anna, when your Mama died Jenny didn't want to bother keeping it and gived it to us?"

My heart jumped.

"Oh, Papa, I sure wouldn't know what happened to that old box after all them years. Might be anywheres—in the back bedroom, the cellar, maybe even the barn."

I found my voice. "You mean you dug up an Indian skeleton from the hill and now you got it hid somewhere?"

Gramma laughed. "An Indian skeleton? Gracious no, Becca! More like a few bits and pieces of deer bone, some long dead Indian's cracked pot, and a few broken shells."

Grampa slowly rubbed his chin. "Oh, I don't know, Anna. From what I remember, those bones was too small for deer. No, I wouldn't doubt that hundreds of years ago that church hill was some kind of Indian burial ground. Why, I remember, when I was just a boy, workmen digging up bones, pieces of pots, and arrowheads before they filled in the church foundation with cement. And I think it must have been old Rhine Zeitema—yeah, that's who it was—he actually found a human jawbone with some teeth still in it. Now that would have been a thing worth saving. Always wondered what he did with that."

"Aw, Papa, don't be filling the child's head with such. Given her imagination, Becca'll have Indian ghosts prowling 'round in the cellar next thing you know."

"Aw, come on, Gramma, I don't believe in ghosts." I swallowed hard. *Well, at least, I hadn't until yesterday. But now there was Wanaga. And I wasn't quite sure what category he fit into. Living or dead?*

His forehead wrinkled in thought, Grampa shook his head. "Still and all, Anna, it'd sure be interesting to know what's really in that box Jenny give us all those years back. Why, today, if somebody happened to dig up those bones, broken clay pots, and whatnot, I dare say there'd be archeologists crawling all over that hill. But way back then… let's see… 1902 it must have been, nobody thought much about those bones and pots, except maybe to keep a piece or two as a curiosity. Wouldn't be surprised if the builders threw most of the relics out, probably just hauled them off to a dump with the rest of the dirt and stones."

"You're going to find the box, Grampa…aren't you?"

"Sure would like to, Becca. You know, Anna, if I do find that box, I'll take it with me next time I get over to Ann Arbor. Ought to be some university professor there would know about such things." He rubbed his chin. "Yeah, that's what I aim to do. Maybe then the university can give it to some museum somewhere."

"Grampa, no! You can't do that!"

Gramma patted my hand. "But why ever not, child?" Gramma asked. "Seems that's the right thing to do. Besides what on earth are Grampa and me going to do with a box of old deer bones and a few chips of broken pottery?"

* * *

I sat on the hard church bench. My collar itched, my backside hurt, and Reverend Holstege had been droning on for over an hour. Each time his voice would drop I prayed the sermon was over, but soon he was building up again to a new crescendo. I scratched at my neck where the lace collar rubbed unmercifully, then watched an iridescent horsefly crawl across the open page of my hymnal, wash his face with tiny front legs, then fly off and light on the daisy sprouting from Mrs. Boersma's pink hat.

Charlene craned her head around and scowled at me. It was hard not to snicker because her pinched lips and evil-eyed squint were a dead ringer for my fifth-grade teacher, Miss Barclay. I thought about returning the gesture but caught Gramma's eyes and decided to wait for a more auspicious time. The hymnbook slipped from my lap and landed with a loud thud on the floor.

Gramma looked sharply at me. "Becca, don't fidget," she hissed. She rummaged through her pocketbook, pulled out a small pink peppermint and handed it to me. As long as I could remember, those peppermints were Gramma's answer to the problem of restless grandchildren, no matter how old, and church. I sucked on the hard mint and sank deep into thought, willing Reverend Holstege to background noise. *There has to be a way to find that box with Sawahna's bones before Grampa does.*

That afternoon, I stood in the back bedroom and peered cautiously through the lace curtains, watching Grampa's car back out of the barn, wind around the driveway, and finally disappear in a cloud of dust down the road. I felt a little guilty that I had to tell Gramma the lie about having a sore throat, but it was that or spend the afternoon at Aunt Mary's. Besides, now that I was alone in the house I was free to search for the box.

The back bedroom seemed as good a place as any to begin. I wrinkled my nose. I never had liked the room's strange, musty, mediciney smell. Though Grampa was now officially retired, relatives and neighbors occasionally called on him to doctor a sick dog, cat, horse, or cow, and he still used the small spare room like he used to, for storing and mixing the drugs he needed. Above a large black dresser hung his gold-framed veterinary diploma, its edges yellow with age.

In a tall corner cabinet, behind glass doors, was an intriguing assortment of bottles, vials, tubes, and cardboard boxes bearing the names of drug companies. Behind the spare bed was a faded flowered curtain that hung from ceiling to floor and covered a closet of shelves. That looked promising. After a mighty struggle, I managed to move the brass bed several inches—enough so I could maneuver between it and the wall. I pushed aside the dusty curtain. Shelf after shelf of old cardboard boxes met my eyes. I sighed. Where to start?

An hour later I had found a checkerboard game, a rusty toy tractor, a cloth-bodied doll with a molded -metal head and black-painted hair, boxes of faded photographs, old clothes, yarn, and dishes, but not the box of Sawahna's bones.

The cellar yielded nothing but row after row of dusty canning jars, a box of Grampa's tools, an old baby carriage, a broken high chair, and a box of yellowing sheet music with little bugs— the ones Gramma called silverfish— crawling over the pile. "Yuck!" I muttered.

Time was fast running out. Soon Gramma and Grampa would be coming home. Flashlight in my pocket, I ran out to the barn and pushed open the heavy sliding door far enough to squeeze in. A shaft of sunlight from the open door sparkled the lazily-floating dust motes into what looked like silver pixie dust. I breathed in the smells— moldering hay, old leather, rusty machinery, and manure. It had been years since Grampa had kept a horse or cow in the two stalls at the rear of the barn, but their ghost scent still lingered.

The gray mother tabby gave a soft meow and rubbed against my leg. Absently, I stooped to pet her. "Well, Minerva," I said, "if you were Gramma, where would you put a box of Indian bones?"

Hands on my hips, I pondered the barn, wall by wall. Hanging from nails were halters, horseshoes, a rusting plow blade, a wagon wheel, covered with cobwebs. Heaped in the far corner were an old bicycle tire, a wagon axle, a dented bucket, and an upside-down, metal washtub. On a high shelf above the junk pile I spied a small wooden chest. I dragged a ladder to the corner, propped it against the shelf, then climbed until I was high enough to reach the chest. Balancing precariously on a rickety rung, I brushed off the layers of dust and slowly opened the lid. Rusty hinges creaked. I took a deep breath and shone the flashlight over its contents.

At first I thought I had found nothing more than a few rocks mixed in with a bunch of gravel. Forcing my hand into the chest, I could feel what had seemed to be only a rock but found it smooth, lightweight, and porous. Hand trembling, I pulled the object out. Could it be a human bone? If it was, the bone was hardly the recognizable piece of a human skeleton I had expected. I pulled out another object. It was a brick-red jagged piece that looked as if it was baked clay, like a broken piece of the mugs we'd made in art class. It had a faded design of black interlocking diamond-shapes. This had to be part of a cooking pot— what Wanaga had called a spirit gift. Swallowing hard, I closed the lid. I had found Sawahna's bones.

FOUR

I parted the branches and entered the clearing. I had debated waiting until the next morning to bring Wanaga the chest, but I wanted to be rid of the bones—as well as Wanaga—forever. Setting the chest on the ground, I dug beneath the pine needles for the necklace he'd promised to leave behind for me. When my fingers touched the polished warmth of the shell pendant, I swallowed hard, my last meeting with Wanaga running through my mind.

I glanced toward the patches of blue sky visible through the branches. Yes, there was yet daylight, but dusk was nearing. In my rush, I had forgotten about the time. Alone with Wanaga at night—that, for sure, was the stuff of nightmares.

Maybe it would be better to just leave the chest under a pine. After all, Gramma and Grampa would soon be home, and I was supposed to be sick in bed with a sore throat. But what if Wanaga never found the chest?

He'd told me that the necklace and my chanted words were the only ways that he could be summoned from his time to mine. If I left the chest under the tree, Charlene or Ben might come snooping around and find it. And Uncle Frank occasionally hunted rabbit in the pines. He might stumble across it. Or even Grampa. Then Sawahna's bones would end up in a museum and never be returned to the Hill of the Dead, where they belonged.

Maybe I should get a shovel from the barn, take the chest back to the church hill and bury the bones and spirit gifts myself? After all, as long as they were returned, did it matter who did the burying? I shuddered, reliving yesterday. "No," I whispered, "I'll never go back to that hill alone."

I glanced toward the patches of deepening blue still visible through the trees. There was enough time left before nightfall, but I had to hurry. Putting on the necklace, I vowed this would be the last time I would summon the grizzly old man. The words to the chant came without struggle this time. A being within me took over my voice and lips. I could only listen.

"Becca," Wanaga hissed.

Looking up with a start, I saw him standing at my side. I could not accustom myself to his sudden appearances and disappearances.

He brushed my cheek with his fingers. "Ah, Little Mouse, so you return to me. Yes, this one last time."

I drew away from him, repulsed by the cold, raspy touch of his fingers. "I...I found the bones." I pushed the chest toward him.

His eyes glowed as he took the chest and slowly raised its lid. He drew out a bone fragment. Holding it close to his eyes, he slowly turned it from back to front. He searched my face in the dusky shadows and gave his raven's cackle. "Little Mouse, you have done well. Ah, yes, very well!"

While he examined the bone fragment, I inched away. At more than an arm's reach from him, I stood. "Well, n...now that you've got Sawahna's bones, guess I...I'll say good-bye."

His expression softened. "But, Becca, we must not forget my gift to you." He pointed toward the necklace which I still wore. "Come kneel here beside me that I may teach you the necklace's sacred medicine."

"Oh, b...but, Wanaga, I'd really rather give it back to you. I don't want to have anything more to do with magic."

I considered hanging on to the necklace until I was as far as the pasture fence, just as I had threatened to do the day before. But since he seemed so eager to give it to me anyway, I thought such a precaution unnecessary. Drawing the necklace over my head, I held it out to him.

"Ah, Becca, if such is your wish, I will take the necklace back, though it saddens me that you refuse my gift." He placed the necklace around his neck.

I saw the nightmarish glow of his eyes, the glint of his yellow teeth in the shadows, and shivered.

"Well, so long, Wanaga. G...guess I'll be going home, now." I made a move to go around him.

With the speed of a striking snake, his arm darted out and grabbed my wrist. "Soon, Little Mouse, we will both go home." He threw back his head and gave a loud laugh.

"Let me go," I screamed, trying to wrench my arm from his grasp. His nails dug deeper into my flesh. "Stop! You're hurting me!"

I pummeled his bare chest with my fist. He grabbed my free wrist and drew me close, so close I could feel the heat of his rank breath against my face.

"Fight," he hissed, "fight like the panther you are, Sawahna, but this time it will be I, the raven, who shall win. Never again will you use your power to defeat me. For now, Sawahna, I possess you in life and in death!"

Placing his hands on my shoulders, he forced me to my knees. "Sawahna, you will obey! And at last, I will triumph!"

Sinking my teeth into his forearm, I tasted the salt of his blood, heard him scream, then felt the blow to my head. All was black.

* * *

At first, I was conscious of nothing but the sharp throbbing in my head, but then I remembered. Wanaga. My throat tightened. Slowly, I opened my eyes, terrified I would see his sharp features, the beady glowing eyes peering into my face. I let out my breath. No Wanaga. Squinting through a gray haze, I could make out what appeared to be the pine trunks that surrounded the clearing. And yet what was that flickering glow? Then I smelled wood smoke, heard the crackle of burning branches. Had Wanaga built a fire in the clearing? I couldn't see clearly.

Thinking my glasses smudged, I took them off, breathed on the lenses and rubbed them on my t-shirt. Then I realized that I could see my fingers and my t-shirt as clearly as if those glasses had been on my face. But how could that be? I put the glasses back on and everything blurred again . Hands trembling, I removed the glasses and again looked around. I couldn't understand why, but suddenly I could see perfectly without glasses.

What I had thought was the pine clearing was actually a dark, circular room. A small fire crackled in a stone-bound hearth. Wisps of smoke spiraled toward a hole in the dome-shaped roof, yet enough smoke remained to give the room its gray haze. What had seemed to be the clearing's pine trees were, instead, the supporting posts for the room's circular walls. I touched the wall behind me. It consisted of overlapping, coarse-woven brown mats similar to the woven doormat that Gramma kept at the back door, except larger. The mats were held in place by crisscrossed saplings. Flush against the walls were three fur-covered, low wooden platforms, exactly like the one on which I was lying. Opposite me, there was a doorway covered with an animal skin. I looked around me in confusion. Overhead hung gourds, animal pelts, a woven bag, a drum, a wooden bowl and soup ladle, string after string of multi-colored ears of corn, and other objects I had never seen before.

Chewing my lip, I fought back the panic and tried to think. *All right, wherever I am, Wanaga must have brought me to this place. He's not here now, but it's for sure he'll be back. And I've got to get out of here.*

I put the useless glasses in a pocket of my jeans and swung my legs over the edge of the platform. Feeling a sharp jerk on my foot, I looked down. My ankle was bound with a length of rope extending from the roof beam far above my head. Frantically, I dug my fingers into the knot but couldn't loosen it. Removing my sneaker, I tried to slide the coarse rope over my foot. I yanked and pushed until the skin on my heel was raw, but I only succeeded in tightening the knot.

Tears beaded down my cheeks. My head ached. The skin of my ankle burned, but I couldn't give up. Any moment, Wanaga could appear. I searched the walls for an object sharp enough to cut through rope. My eyes lit on the drum, its edge decorated with what appeared to be dangling shells. A shell's edge might be sharp enough to slice through the tough fibers of the rope. But how to reach the drum hanging from that beam yards away? I stood, legs spread-eagled as far as the rope would allow and extended my arm. As though bent on tantalizing me, the drum dangled a mere foot from my fingertips.

Sinking back onto the platform, I examined my bloody ankle. I felt a knot of fear rising in my throat, threatening to explode into screams. Then it occurred to me. Of course, my glasses. Why, all I have to do is break a lens. What could be sharper than a piece of broken glass?

I reached into my pocket for the glasses. My fingers froze around the frame when I heard muffled voices. There was no doubt the raspy voice was Wanaga's. In Akwanakai he was talking to someone just outside the skin-covered doorway. He pushed aside the skin flap and entered, with another man close behind him. For an instant, sunlight flooded the wigwam before the flap dropped back over the doorway, shrouding the interior again in hazy shadows. Shielding my head with my arms, I curled my body into a tense ball and listened.

"Well, Nowuk, there's the girl." The voice was Wanaga's. "No more than a worthless Iroquois girl-child, but, alas, all that I could afford."

The other man snorted a laugh. "I fear, Wanaga, the Huron with whom you traded got the better of the bargain. Looks like a mere mite of a girl. Hard work will kill her off long before she reaches womanhood. Why do you not seek among our women a wife, perhaps a widow, who could warm your bed at night and care for you, not just a child to do your work?"

Wanaga gave a cackling laugh. " Ay, Nowuk, I am an old man. I have no desire for bedding a woman anymore. Ah, but this child, do not fear. She will work for me and serve my purposes well."

Hearing the muffled whisper of moccasins on the hard-dirt floor, I peered up through my arms and saw a tall, bare-chested Indian looming over me. I cringed into a tighter ball as he reached down and fingered first the hem of my t-shirt, then the denim waistband of my jeans.

"Wanaga, what are these strange leggings and shirt your slave wears? They are like no woven cloth or animal skin I have ever seen."

"Ah, that. Take no notice. The Huron stole her away from the Iroquois only one, maybe two, moons ago, and still she wears her people's strange robes."

"Heh, Wanaga, very strange robes, indeed."

The tall man wrapped his fingers around my upper arm and gently squeezed. When I whimpered and pulled away, his expression softened as though he wanted to tell me with his eyes not to fear him.

"Ay! Way too thin," he muttered, the brusqueness in his voice strangely at odds with the kindness in his face. Appearing to ponder the situation, the man rubbed his chin.

"Perhaps, Wanaga, I could relieve you of the burden of this… well, unfortunate purchase. Maybe my woman could put to good use an Iroquois captive, even such a puny, worthless child as this."

My heart leapt with hope.

"No, the girl is mine!" Wanaga snarled.

"Of course, Wanaga, of course," the man said, his voice immediately placating.

Abruptly he turned from me, and my hopes this man might rescue me crumbled.

Wanaga gestured to the man to sit before the fire. "Now, to business— the warrior's amulet. Do we strike a bargain or not?"

"You guarantee, Wanaga, that this amulet will turn aside my enemies' arrows?"

"Ayah, but of course! It is a certainty."

The man thought a moment, then spoke, "A bear robe, a quiver of arrows, and a length of finest buckskin. That is my offer."

"Ay, Nowuk, you insult my medicine. For such I would not give you so much as a woman's love charm. No, my friend, we speak here of an amulet that will render you an invincible warrior."

The bargaining went on until they reached a mutually acceptable price. They clasped forearms. Wanaga took a woven bag from a peg and drew out a small, embroidered pouch. Handing it to the man, Wanaga said, "Remember, Nowuk, my instructions. Heed them well, or the amulet is useless."

The man gave an abrupt nod. "The skins, the arrows, Wanaga. All I shall bring to your wigwam upon tomorrow's sunrise, as we agreed."

Seeing the man walk toward the doorway, I bolted to a sitting position and called out, "Wait, please, Mr. Nowuk, sir! Take me with you. I'll work for your wife. I'll do anything. Just don't leave me here with Wanaga."

Nowuk gave a sad shake of his head. "What strange gibberish your little Iroquois speaks. How will you ever teach her to speak as a human and not with such a twisted tongue?"

Wanaga looked toward me, his smile an evil leer. "Ah, Nowuk, she will learn. My Little Mouse will learn."

I covered my head with my arms. Wanaga waited until Nowuk left, then walked to the platform where I lay and stooped to examine my ankle. "Ah, so you've been up to mischief while I was gone. Bloodied your ankle, have you?" He reached out as if to touch my foot. "My poor Sawahna."

I slapped away his hand and scrambled as far from him as the rope would allow. "Where am I?"

"You told me you wished to return home." He reared back his head and laughed. "So I granted your wish, Sawahna. Now you are home, returned at last to the Akwanakai."

"You don't make any sense! And why do you keep calling me Sawahna?"

"Because, Little Mouse, you are Sawahna."

"No...NO. I'm Becca Morrison. My Gramma and Grampa know I play in these pines. You can't keep me here. It won't be long and they'll come looking for me."

"The ones you call Gramma and Grampa—they exist in another time. Hundreds of winters must pass before they will even be born. Besides, if they were able to travel through time as we did, they would never recognize you as their granddaughter."

He took a six-inch disk of polished copper from a niche in the wall and held it before my eyes. I looked into the rippled reflection and an almond-eyed Indian girl stared back at me.

"NO, NO!" I sobbed. "This is just another one of your tricks." To reassure myself, I touched one of my braids. But it felt too thick to be mine. I held the braid so I could see it. The color was glossy black, not brown.

Wanaga held his arm flush to mine. "Our skin color— do you see a difference now?"

With a sob, I buried my head in my hands. "I'm not me anymore! What did you do to me?"

"Remember when I told you Sawahna's spirit wandered lost through time? You are that spirit. I have returned you to the body you once possessed as an Akwanakai child. I have done you a favor, Sawahna. Ten winters ago, you died, a bent and shriveled old woman. Now, here you are again a young girl." His lips curled into an evil sneer. "Yes, the girl I remember so well and even loved."

My voice quivered. "But...I watched them bury that woman you called Sawahna in the church hill."

"And so they did. Ah, so much you have forgotten. But, I? No, you will find Wanaga has not forgotten. I tell you now, you will live to curse the day you humiliated me before the council of elders, making me seem the fool. You called into question my medicine powers, saying I used them only for evil. Those wounds you once dealt me, Sawahna, have too long festered, but now, at last, I have the means to lance my wounds clean. I will have the power you once had."

As he spoke, he drew closer. I cowered, back to the wall, my trembling fingers clutching the fur robe tighter around my shoulders.

"But, my dear Sawahna, can it be you do not remember that once we were as brother and sister, learning together the sacred medicine way of our ancestors?" He snorted a laugh. "You thought you surpassed me when the Holy Man chose to bestow his sacred power and all its secrets upon you, rather than me. Always you suspected I used my medicine power to murder your warrior husband, didn't you? Well, perhaps...just perhaps I did. Love often turns to hate, you know, and demands revenge. What a pity for you, because if it had only been I that had been chosen, our paths would not have crossed this second—and, for you I'm afraid, this final—time. But you went too far, Sawahna, when you dared to not only surpass my medicine powers, but also to humiliate me."

"I never did anything to you. I never even knew you until I saw you that day in my grandpa's pines."

"Poor, foolish Sawahna. Why, how could you forget the whole lifetime we lived as rivals within the same village?" The disdainful grin faded and his face twisted with rage. "Winter after long winter, I watched your medicine grow stronger in the eyes of the people. The day finally came when I could bear the shame no longer. Do you remember better now?"

I sunk further into the robe. "How can I remember something that never happened?"

His lips curled into a snarl. "Have no doubt...never, never will I forget that day. Oh, I was foolhardy, to have challenged your medicine power before the council. I see that now, but challenge you, I did. And merely defeating me was not enough for you, Sawanha. You humiliated me without mercy. I never forgave you that deed. But it wasn't until many winters later, when I watched them lay you in your grave, that I saw how I might achieve the perfect revenge. I could steal your power and make it my own. To that end, I came that very night, dug up your body, and took from your withered neck the panther necklace, believing it to be the source of your medicine. Ah, but I was wrong. In time, I realized I also needed to possess your spirit. Through the centuries, you eluded me until that day when I sensed your spirit-presence in the place you call the pines.

"Now, revenge was in my grasp. I had but to capture your spirit and draw it back through time. To do that, I needed to possess your bones as well as your necklace.

Alas, White Men had stolen your bones from the Hill of the Dead. Then, my foolish Little Mouse, you were kind enough to assist me, to bring me your own bones." His cackle grew into a roar of laughter. "And, now, at long last, I possess your spirit. Your youth, your vitality, the power you once possessed as the medicine woman Sawahna. I will bleed them into my own withering body. As you sicken and finally die, so I shall grow strong."

I pressed my hands over my ears. "No, I won't listen to you. This is crazy!"

A sneer on his face, he clucked his tongue in mock dismay. "Ah, Sawahna, such a pity your spirit-memory is so faint. But then, perhaps, that will be all the better for my purpose."

FIVE

Huddled in the farthest corner of the sleeping platform, I watched Wanaga stir the contents of the clay pot that rested in the hearth's coals. The strong spoiled-meat smell made my stomach churn.

He glanced up and caught my gaze. His face crinkled into a sneer. "Ah, Little Mouse, awake at last." He ladled the steaming broth into a small wooden bowl and held it out toward me.

I gave an emphatic shake of my head. "No! I don't want anything you give me."

"What a shame. For beaver soup makes the blood grow strong." He slurped down the contents of the bowl and gave a loud burp. "Ah, no matter. You'll change your mind soon enough, when hunger begins to gnaw at your belly."

"No, I won't, not ever! Whatever that stuff was that you made me drink last night, it made me dizzy, and now my head hurts."

"But, Little Mouse, that was merely tea made from healing herbs. That open sore on your ankle festers. Foolish to keep pulling on the rope the way you do. Only tightens the knot." He gave a rusty chuckle. "Don't want to be buried a second time so soon, do you, Sawahna?"

I clenched my fists and screamed, "I'm not Sawahna. And I'm not Little Mouse. My name is Becca Morrison!"

He laughed, first a little, then harder and harder. "No more than a panther kitten, yet already you hiss and lash out with claws bared. Sawahna, how little you have changed. I salute you."

I held myself rigid. "You can't keep me here. Not forever. You'll see. Someday, I'll get away."

"And where will you go?"

His question hit me like a blow. If Wanaga had indeed somehow taken me back in time hundreds of years—and I was beginning to believe he had—where would I go? My mother, father, baby brother, Gramma, Grampa, everyone I loved—they weren't even born yet. Rage dissolved into despair. I chewed my lip to keep from crying. "I'll find someone who'll help me."

"When you find this person who'll help you, what will you tell him?"

I forced my eyes to his. "I'll tell him you...you kidnapped me, and...that I'm from another time."

"And how do you propose to tell him this?"

"What do you mean, 'how'? I just will."

His lips curled into an evil smile. "The way yesterday you told Nowuk you would work for his wife, if only he would take you from my wigwam?" He gave a loud laugh. "Do you forget so quickly, Little Mouse? Nowuk understood nothing of what you said. He heard only your White Man's gibberish."

My lip trembled. "But I understood everything he said."

"Long ago I opened your ears to the Akwanakai tongue. You will understand what others say, but none will understand you."

"But you do."

"My medicine is strong. I have the ability to open my ears to your White Man's tongue."

I swiped at the tears dripping down my cheek. "I'll find a way to make them understand."

"Oh, Little Mouse, people will 'understand,' but only what I have chosen for them to understand. If you recall, I told Nowuk that you were an Iroquois captive."

I gave a loud sniff.

"The Iroquois have long been enemies of the Akwanakai. They attack our villages with the fire sticks given them by the White Men. They burn our fields and wigwams, steal our women and children, and murder our young men. When the Iroquois last raided, Akwanakai warriors trailed their war party and attacked them as they slept. Most they killed where they lay, but our warriors brought two back alive to the village." Eyes glowing evilly, he licked his lips with relish. "Do you know, Little Mouse, what happened to those two Iroquois captives?"

"No."

"Ah, but you should know what to expect because you are an Iroquois captive, too. Well, now, let me see... as I remember, they bound each captive to a post. The woman who had lost the most relatives to the Iroquois got to choose which part— an ear, a nose, a hand, a foot— would be cut off first. While the captive watched, the woman roasted his body part over the fire, then threw it to the dogs. After that, the next woman got her chance. Piece by piece those warriors died. Takes a long time, you know, when it's done right. Ah, brave men, those two Iroquois were. Not once did they cry out. What about you, Little Mouse? Will you cry out?"

"But those captives were men. They wouldn't do that to a girl."

"Perhaps, you're right. They might show you mercy and decide to burn you alive instead. Though, remember, Little Mouse, breathe the smoke deeply. You'll die faster that way."

I stifled a sob. "You're just trying to scare me."

"Think what you will." He gave a shrug, then leaned toward me, his black eyes glittering with reflected firelight. "But remember, now I am your protector. Nowuk has spread the word throughout the village that you are my slave. None would dare harm the property of Wanaga. But run from me and I will declare you an escaped Iroquois captive. Then, by Akwanakai law, you will be condemned to die."

* * *

Day melted into day. The smoke hole in the domed roof was the only way I could tell day from night. In the evening, I glimpsed the stars. Wanaga, sitting cross-legged before the flickering fire, carved an amulet from a small wood chunk. As he hunched over his work, he chanted, his voice rising and falling in an eerie trill. The panther necklace glinted pearl against the copper skin of his chest. Shadows like little gnomes danced on the wigwam walls as though the old man had called them forth with his chant. He glanced toward me and I scrunched my eyes shut. He thought I was asleep, but I could just catch the meaning of his muttering over the crackling noise of the fire.

"Ah, Little Mouse, you are still Sawanha, but now I have you trapped in the body of this weakling girl. Know that I am too wise to truly harm you in any way now and also wise enough to confront your power when I am ready. So do not deceive yourself. I will wear you down. I will take from you the strength and power that is rightfully mine. Yes, you will be an even more pitiful wretch, and I shall throw you away like the empty shell of a locust."

Each day, when I glimpsed a patch of blue through the smoke hole and sunlight misted the smoke in the wigwam to silver haze, I knew another morning had begun. Using my fingernail, I carved a small notch into the sapling that held the wall mat in place. There were three notches now in that sapling. Three notches—three days. Yet sometimes I had the disturbing feeling that an entire day had passed me by—a day of which I had only an incoherent, dream-like recollection.

Sleep seemed to come and go with unpredictable suddenness since Wanaga had kidnapped me. And with sleep came the dreams, or were they vague memories? There was the recurring dream that Wanaga held the rope tied to my ankle and led me from the wigwam like a dog on a leash. At first the sunlight had blinded me, I remembered. After my eyes adjusted to the bright light, I saw trees like skyscrapers looming above me. Wanaga and I stood before a river. The sound of a rushing stream rang in my ears. I recalled holding a bucket and filling it with water so icy my fingers tingled. In another dream, I was again bound by Wanaga's leash and carried load after heavy load of branches back to the wigwam. Were these dreams or reality?

I couldn't decide. So many of my dreams seemed real. There were dreams from which I didn't want to wake… those were the dreams of home. Several nights ago, I was snuggling under crisp, white sheets, still smelling faintly of bleach. The walls of the wigwam had vanished, and surrounding me were the pink-flowered walls of my bedroom back home in Chicago. Mama tiptoed in, stooped to kiss my cheek and whispered, "Goodnight, Becca. We love you."

And in my latest dream I had been sneaking down the basement stairs, terrified that when I reached the bottom step Wanaga would be there waiting in ambush. But, no, there was Daddy standing at his workbench. When he turned I ran into his outstretched arms and buried my face against his chest. While he rocked me in his arms I breathed deeply the smell of sawdust and pipe smoke that was Daddy. But when he began to speak I awakened.

And there, all about me, were once again the smoke-blackened walls of the wigwam. As always when I had awakened from a long sleep, I felt that familiar, pounding ache in my head and experienced the sour metallic taste in my mouth. It had happened so many times before. I knew if I tried to sit upright too quickly, the wigwam walls would spin into a kaleidoscope of muted brown, gray, and black. Wanaga had told me that the dizziness, the headache, and the sour taste were all symptoms of my fever. But I didn't feel hot and, besides, the open sore on my ankle was healing, not getting worse.

Burning tears welled in my eyes. Home, the people who loved me… would I now see them only in dreams? I pulled the musky fur robe over my head to shut out the walls of the wigwam and Wanaga's evil leer. Slipping my hand into one of the pockets in my jeans I fingered my glasses. They were my hope for escape. A broken glasses lens…that rope on my ankle. All I needed was time alone.

But that never happened. Always, it seemed, Wanaga was there. Logic told me he had to leave the wigwam at some time. I knew he must. Why, just the day before I had awakened and he was scraping the skin of a freshly killed deer. And every day fresh water was in the bucket. Firewood appeared in a neatly stacked pile just inside the entrance, when it seemed only minutes before there had been none. Beside my sleeping platform was the pot where I relieved myself. The stench would grow overpowering and the pot would threaten to overflow, then suddenly I would find it emptied. But always, always, when I was awake, Wanaga was there.

I heard the muffled croak of his voice through the robe's heavy thickness. "Little Mouse, the soup is ready. Good fresh deer meat this time."

I pressed my hands over my ears to block out his voice. "I don't want any."

Wanaga flung the robe from my head. "Dare you defy me? You will drink. Now!" He jerked my hands away from my ears.

Eyes tightly shut, I gripped the robe's long black fur between my fingers. "I won't. I won't!" I screamed, tensing for a blow.

Instead, I felt him sit on the sleeping platform and stroke my hand. His voice softened as though he were a kindly grandfather cajoling a child. "Now, Becca, you know your fever will only grow worse if you do not eat. And see…I have made the soup rich with deer chunks and the last of the dried squash. Smell, child." He held the wooden bowl near my nose and chanted in a soft hissing sing-song, "Hungry. You are hungry, Becca. So hungry…so very hungry." Over and over, he repeated the words.

His chant melted into my brain, smothering first my rage, then my thoughts. Now why was it I hadn't wanted to drink Wanaga's soup? I had forgotten the reason. After all, I was hungry and the soup smelled so good. I let him raise me to a sitting position. Slowly opening my eyes, I saw my hands reaching for the bowl of steaming broth.

"Ah, now, there's a good Little Mouse, and Grandfather Wanaga has much to do today." With a cackling chuckle, he patted my cheek and turned away.

His back toward me, he squatted before the fire and emptied the contents of his medicine bag on the wigwam's hard dirt floor. Muttering under his breath, he began sifting through the bag's assortment of pebbles, tiny bones, and feathers.

I touched the bowl's rim to my lips. The smell of the meat broth made my mouth water, but I hesitated, Wanaga's muttering beginning to seep into my consciousness. Wanaga…broth…there was something important I had to remember about the two. But what was it? I took a tentative sip. No, I must not drink it. I spit it back into the bowl and sat immobile with my fingers clutching the bowl, groping for thoughts that trembled just out of reach.

Moments passed. The heat of the bowl began burning my fingers. *Pain...danger...Wanaga.* As the three slowly intertwined in my mind, memory and thought returned.

Have to escape. Drink the broth and I will sleep. No, this time stay awake. I must!

I glanced at the cup filled to the brim, then to where Wanaga hunkered over his magic objects. My eyes skittered over the walls, the sleeping platform, the dirt floor, until they lit on the half-full pot I used as a toilet. I eased myself to the sleeping platform's edge and reaching down, slowly poured the broth into the pot, never once taking my eyes from Wanaga. Unaware of my actions, he continued his sing-song mutterings.

After dipping my finger in the nearly empty cup, I smeared a little of the broth on my lips, then sank back onto the platform and closed my eyes. Long minutes passed. I heard the shuffle of his moccasins on the floor and held my breath. Fighting the urge to cringe, I endured the stench of his rank breath as he stooped to peer into my face and sniff at my lips. I forced my body to go limp when I felt him take the bowl from my hand and poke his bony finger into my side.

He gave out with a loud laugh. "Sleep, Sawahna, long and hard."

When I heard him rummaging through the food baskets on the opposite side of the wigwam, I opened one eye no wider than a slit. I watched as he loaded the food into his pack, slung it over his shoulders, and grabbed for his bow and quiver of arrows. Glancing over his shoulder at me, he gave a satisfied grunt and started for the entrance. As though he had suddenly remembered something, he paused with his hand on the fur robe that covered the doorway. Turning, he stepped to the wall, removed the panther necklace from his neck and hung it on a peg. For a moment, he held the shell in his hand, then tenderly brushed it against his lips.

I don't know how long I lay there rigid after he left. Finally I mustered the courage to sit up and glance around uneasily. Wanaga had banked the fire before he left. Only a few wisps of smoke spiraled toward the patch of blue showing through the smoke hole.

I pulled out my glasses and stared at them. This was the moment I had been waiting for. I was alone. Yet why couldn't I now do what I had rehearsed over and over in my mind?

Wanaga's words rang in my ears. "The woman roasted the Iroquois captive's body part over the fire and then threw it to the dogs while he looked on. And, what about you, Little Mouse? Will you cry out?"

I swallowed hard and threw my glasses on the packed-dirt floor. With a mighty stomp of my free foot, I shattered one of the lenses. Carefully, I examined the glass shards and chose the sharpest one. As I sliced back and forth over the tough rope fibers, I tried to calm my fears, or at least justify the danger of escape. While I was trapped in Wanaga's wigwam I had no chance, but out there maybe, just maybe, I would find a way to return home.

When the last rope fiber fell away from my ankle, I looked toward the doorway, terrified that at any moment Wanaga, his face twisted with rage, would appear. Unable to part with any bit of my former life, even those hated glasses, I picked up the broken frame with its one remaining lens still intact and returned the glasses to my pocket. I forced myself to stand. My jeans and T-shirt hung two sizes too big on this new body I had. Even though my clothes must reek by now I had nothing else to wear and even if I had other clothes I didn't want to part with anything from my real life. The walls of the wigwam spun. I stood immobile until the dizziness subsided.

Concentrating on putting one foot in front of the other, I walked shakily toward the center of the wigwam. I scanned the walls, looking for items I might need for my escape, the provisions that would enable me to survive for days in the forest, if necessary. My eyes lit on the panther necklace. Was it, I wondered, the necklace that had allowed Wanaga to travel through time? If that were true, I needed that necklace to return to the twentieth century and home.

Hands shaking, I walked to the wall, pulled the necklace from its peg and slipped it over my head. I felt the pendant's strange tingling warmth against my breast bone. Hesitantly, I ran my fingers over the panther carved onto the shell. What was it Wanaga had said? Sawahna's power was in her necklace... and also in her spirit? I raised my chin. Neither Wanaga nor the Akwanakai could stop me. I was going to find home.

I pushed aside the robe a crack and peered cautiously into the bright sunlight. I edged further and further out of the doorway, finally letting the robe fall behind me. Over my shoulder, I carried a coarsely woven bag bulging with my plunder from Wanaga's wigwam— dried pumpkin, withered strips of meat, and corn ears studded with hard rainbow-colored kernels. Wedged amongst the food was the knife Wanaga used to whittle his amulets.

I let out the breath I had been holding. There were no other wigwams in sight. The presence of other Akwanakai had been my greatest fear, short of encountering Wanaga. I suspected his wigwam was far from the village, for I had never heard voices other than my own and Wanaga's. And, except for Nowuk on that first day, he'd had no visitors.

His wigwam stood alone in a small clearing surrounded by maples and elms with trunks larger than any I had ever seen. The trees' uppermost limbs were hazed pale green with new leaves and appeared to scrape the clouds. Birds twittered and drifted among their branches.

I stretched my arms up and breathed in the cool breeze, sweet with moist earth and growing things. I was free— free forever from Wanaga and his smoky, dark cage. But, now, where to go? To one side was a path, although it more closely resembled a black tunnel leading off into the forest. Should I take it? I gave an emphatic shake of my head. No, I had seen too many movies to make the obvious mistake of taking a well-defined path.

I headed in the opposite direction from the path and entered the dense forest. Weaving my way through the tangled underbrush, I tried not to break any branches. I avoided the patches of moist bare earth and the young plants that would bruise, stepping only where the thick carpet of dead leaves would absorb my footprints and leave no imprint.

Pausing to look behind me, I gave a smug smile. *Well, all those years of pretending to be an Indian has paid off. There's no sign I can see that I've given my trail away.*

As the sun climbed, the euphoria of being free began wearing off and hunger gnawed at my stomach. I pulled a strip of meat from the bag. It didn't taste bad, but it had the consistency of the rawhide dog chews Mama bought for Skipper. Swiping at the tear on my cheek, I blocked out the vision of the shaggy, brown mutt. I had to think now, not cry.

My goal was to put as much distance as possible between me and Wanaga, as well as any other Akwanakai in the vicinity. To avoid backtracking I had been keeping the sun over my right shoulder. Or, at least, I had been trying to. I had to search out breaks in the thick tree cover in order to see the sun and get my bearings. But now that the sun was almost directly overhead, I wasn't sure which direction I was going. "Oh, God," I whispered, "I can't be walking in a circle. Please, not back to Wanaga's wigwam."

Step after step grew into mile after mile. I stumbled now among the bushes, not caring if I broke branches. I barely noticed the thorns that tore at my clothes and scratched my arms. The position of the sun was no longer a concern. I was thirsty. All I could think of was water. Over and over, I played out those moments in the wigwam when I had scavenged in the baskets for food, hunted for Wanaga's knife. Not once had I thought about taking a container of water. Now I conjured the vision of that bucket of cool delicious water and imagined how it would feel trickling down my throat.

How could I have been that stupid? Why, I practically had to step over that water bucket to get out the doorway. I sniffed back a sob and stumbled on.

At first the sound blended deceptively with the wind and the twittering birds. Then unmistakably I heard it, the gurgling murmur of rushing water. I followed the sound to a spot where the forest opened onto a stream fringed with reeds. The breeze gusted and points of light danced on the water's rippling surface. Flinging down my bag, I ran for the stream and knelt in the reeds. I cupped my hands and, scattering a school of tiny, silvery fish, I greedily scooped up the icy water. After I quenched my thirst, I focused on the rippling reflection in the stream. A pretty, brown-eyed, copper-skinned girl stared back. Disheveled black braids hung past her shoulders.

I choked back a sob. "I'm me," I said to the shimmering reflection, my voice trembling. "Not Sawahna, not Little Mouse. I'm ME, Becca Morrison."

I struggled back through the reeds to the grassy bank and collapsed, pillowing my head on my arm. I sobbed until no more tears would come. I knew I ought to keep walking, but I was too exhausted. My feet were sore and my head ached with the effort of keeping my eyes open. My legs were lifeless stumps. *I'll only rest here for a little while,* I promised myself, then closed my eyes.

* * *

I bolted to a sitting position, eyes wide with panic. I had dreamt I was back at Wanaga's wigwam. Now, heart pounding, I took in the stream, the dense forest behind me, the sun low in the sky. I was still free, though the nightmare made me more cautious. I knew that for the last few miles I had been careless about leaving a trail.

My eyes lit on the stream. *Of course, in movies the Indian scout always covered his tracks by walking through a stream.* But my reflected image in the stream came back to me. *If I wade through the water, with every step I'll see the stranger's body Wanaga has imprisoned me in.* I swallowed the knot in my throat.

So I look different, but I'm still Becca inside. And, whatever else happens, I can't let Wanaga capture me again. I can't.

I removed my sneakers, tied the laces together and fastened them to the top strap of my bag. After rolling up my jeans, I stood and walked toward the stream. As I parted the reeds, I heard a loud snort. A dark shape rushed at me, its coarse fur grazing my legs. I screamed and jumped into the reeds. My foot hit a rock. I stumbled and fell face first into the stream. The icy water burned. I fought the fast, swirling current to regain my footing, but when I put weight on my foot, a sharp pain shot through my ankle. I hobbled from the water and pulled myself on hands and knees up the sandy bank. I tried again to put weight on the foot but doubled over in pain.

Fighting tears, I limped a little further onto the bank and massaged my ankle. My eyes darted anxiously from the nearby clump of bushes toward the rippling reeds, toward the dark forest looming behind me. Whatever animal had charged between my legs had vanished.

The wind grew cold. Shadows crept from the reeds and forest as though sniffing me before deciding to devour me. I shivered from fear as much as from cold. Not only had I forgotten a water container but I'd left the robe behind, too. How I had hated the stench of the fur robe Wanaga had given me, but now I would have welcomed the smell, buried my nose in the rank black fur, just to feel it wrap my body in its warmth.

I glanced toward the forest. Maybe within the cover of the trees it would not be as cold. I hobbled toward the forest's shadowy murk. I paused at the first line of trees, my hand clutching the necklace's shell pendant. It was so dark in there— wolves, bears, maybe even a panther stalked its shadows. But the cold was greater than the fear. I entered the forest, slumped down at the foot of a huge maple and leaned my back against its trunk.

I slept fitfully while the night passed. Intruding into my dream was the persistent sound of a girl's voice, faint at first, then growing louder and more difficult to ignore. I felt a gentle shaking of my shoulders. My eyes jerked open, and a dark face peered into my own.

The face smiled. "Do not be afraid," the girl said in Akwanakai. She touched her chest shyly. "I am called Nemisa."

SIX

I shrank from the girl. Using the tree trunk as a brace, I
tried to stand. Pain shot through my ankle and, with a
whimper, I crumpled to the ground. Squeezing my eyes
shut, I curled into a tight ball tensing for whatever horrible
thing was about to happen. But there was no rush of feet,
no loud, angry voices, just the soft gurgle of the stream and
the plaintive call of a mourning dove. Cautiously, I opened
my eyes, expecting that the girl must have run off to bring
reinforcements.

But she was still there, a girl close in years to me,
though several inches shorter. Wrapped in a robe of what
looked like many sewn-together rabbit skins, the girl's face,
round and full-cheeked, was the only part of her visible.
When her black, almond eyes met mine she looked shyly
away.

She squatted before me and examined my ankle.
"You've hurt your foot?"

I gave a limp nod, as my teeth began to chatter. A cold
gust of wind rattled the branches and I shivered, my clothes
still damp from my fall in the stream.

"And you're cold, too," the girl said, concern in her
voice. "Surely, those strange robes you wear don't keep

you warm." Hesitantly, she fingered the denim of my jeans. When she realized I was watching her, she jerked her hand away. "Here, wear my robe until your leggings dry." She slipped the fur robe from her shoulders and placed it around mine.

Sinking into the robe's warmth, I began to say "Thank you," but stopped, remembering the girl wouldn't understand anyway. Looking up, I hoped to say with my expression what words could not communicate. My eyes lit on her hand, withered like a crab's pincers and consisting of only a thumb and two fingers. It extended from the sleeve of her fringed deerskin shirt at the point where her elbow should have joined to her forearm. She followed my eyes and made a flustered move with her normal arm to shield her deformity.

"Please, don't fear me. I am no evil-spirit, no forest manitou. I was born of my mother this way. My foot, too." She extended a foot. "It is misshapen and joined crooked to my leg. Though outside my body is twisted," she touched her chest, "inside you'll find my spirit is whole." When I didn't respond, she gave a sigh and shook her head. "Ah, what a fool I am. You understand nothing of what I say, do you?"

"Oh, but I do," I said, making a grab for the girl's normal hand, desperate to keep what seemed to be a possible friend. I pointed to my own chest. "Becca," I said, then pointed to the girl, praying I remembered her name correctly. "Ne–mi-sa."

Breaking into a broad grin, the girl gave my hand a squeeze. "So you do understand a little? But Nowuk told us you spoke only Iroquois."

I gave an emphatic shake of my head. "No," I said, continuing with exaggerated slowness in English. "Becca." I pointed to myself. "Becca not Iroquois…not…**not** Iroquois!" I shook my head again to get my point across.

Nemisa gave my hand a sympathetic pat. "Ah, yes, I know you are an Iroquois captive. It must be a terrible thing to be captured and then, even worse, to be sold to such an evil one as Wanaga. Me, I'm lucky. Your people wouldn't bother kidnapping a girl with twisted limbs. They would kill me, I know. But better that than be carried off to live a slave among enemies, as you have been."

Visions of tortured captives whirled through my head as I cast about for a way to explain I wasn't Iroquois. Last year, I had read a book about Indian sign language, but now all I could remember were the signs for setting sun, teepee, and papoose, none of which seemed especially helpful at the moment.

Nemisa stood and, giving a loud sigh, said, "Well, I certainly can't leave you here."

My eyes went wide with fear.

"Oh, don't be afraid," Nemisa said, stooping to pick up a large cord-bound bundle of branches. "I'll take you to Grandmother, not back to Wanaga." Steadying the bundle with her deformed arm, she managed to maneuver it to her back. She looked to me. "Could you help me hold the bundle until I get the burden strap on my forehead?"

Immobilized with fear, I sat tightly clutching the robe around me. Go to an Akwanakai village? But what if all the things Wanaga had said about his people's cruelty were true?

"Becca?" Nemisa said slowly and distinctly as if she were talking to a young child. "You...help...me?" She jerked her head toward the wood bundle on her back, then stepped closer so I could reach it without standing.

I looked up with a nervous start. "Oh, yeah, the branches...sure." Absently, I reached up and supported the bundle while Nemisa put across her forehead an embroidered strap that attached to the cord-bound firewood. All the while I was estimating my chances of out-hobbling the crippled girl. *But then, what's the point?*

How far could I get before the girl fetches warriors to find me? I studied Nemisa, her smile friendly on a face round as a copper penny, thick, glossy-black braids falling to her waist. I want to trust her. I have to. There's no other choice.

Nemisa adjusted the burden strap with her good arm while continuing her one-sided conversation. "Grandmother, you know, days ago, took pity on you. When she saw Nowuk was bound for Wanaga's wigwam to bargain for a war amulet, she told him 'Try to buy that captive girl of Wanaga's. No child, not even an Iroquois, should be given to such an evil one. Tell him your woman has need of a slave, so he doesn't suspect your true motives.'"

Nemisa clucked her tongue in dismay. "Ah, too bad Wanaga reacted with such anger. Nowuk told us he didn't dare persist in bargaining for you. It was obvious Wanaga was not willing to part with you for any price." Nemisa's face clouded, and she glanced anxiously behind her. "If you ran away—and surely you must have—Wanaga will be very angry. Even now he probably searches for you."

I had been fighting tears, but now a sob escaped me.

"Come, we must leave here quickly," Nemisa said, extending her good arm toward me to help me stand. "Grandmother, more than any other, can protect you from Wanaga."

With a groan, I stood, one hand clutching Nemisa's arm, the other the robe around my shoulders.

"Go ahead," Nemisa said, "just lean on me. I may not look it, but I'm strong. Have to drag my bad foot a little, but I manage."

I winced with pain when I put my weight on my ankle.

"And, don't worry, Grandmother will be able to heal that sore foot, too. She is a medicine woman of great power. Many say even greater than Wanaga."

I drew back in alarm. I'd had enough of Indian medicine and magic.

Nemisa noted my reaction and gave me a smile meant to reassure. "Oh, no need to fear Grandmother's medicine, for it is good, not evil. Why, when my mother died at my birth, they intended to bury me in her grave as well, but Grandmother forbade it. Instead, she took me home to her wigwam and has cared for me ever since." Nemisa cocked her head and pondered me. "I wonder... do you understand anything of what I'm saying?"

I began to nod but, suddenly, my face contorted with pain. My bare foot had hit a sharp rock.

Nemisa stooped to examine the wound. "What a pity you have no moccasins. Your feet will be bleeding badly long before we reach the village."

She placed her normal foot beside mine. "I would give you one of my moccasins for your good foot but, see, your foot is so much bigger. It would never fit."

Urgently, I gestured toward the stream bank where I had left the bag with my shoes tied to its strap.

"Oh, no," Nemisa said, "that's the wrong way. We must go this way, toward the village."

I stood fast, pointed to my feet, then gestured toward the stream.

"What? Oh, you have moccasins over there?"

I nodded vigorously.

I found Wanaga's bag in the reeds, my sneakers still tied by their shoelaces to the bag's strap. While I put on one soggy shoe, Nemisa curiously examined the other. She brushed her fingers over the canvas, then sniffed at the sole, wrinkling her nose at the rubber smell. Her eyes went wide as she touched the shiny, metal rings edging the shoelace holes.

She handed the sneaker to me and said, awe in her voice, "Never have I seen such strange moccasins. Not even on other Iroquois captives."

I winced at the reference to Iroquois captives, but forced myself to focus on getting the second shoe over my injured foot. After several tries, I gave up. My foot was too swollen. I tied the shoe back onto the bag. After Nemisa had shouldered the wet pack and sneaker, I leaned on her good arm and we both hobbled back into the forest, this time following a well-marked path.

On and on the path meandered among towering maples and elms. Finally, above the chirping of the birds, I heard the distant sound of dogs barking. We passed more twists of the trail, and I saw wisps of smoke spiraling above the treetops. My hands grew cold, moist with fear. The path widened, and I began to hear the faint buzz of women's voices, then the shriek of children's laughter. A man called out in a deep, booming voice. I froze, my legs refusing to take another step. I pulled the robe around my head to make a deep hood, my eyes casting about for somewhere I could hide.

Nemisa urged me on with a gentle tug. "Come. Grandmother won't let them hurt you."

The forest opened onto a large clearing dotted with many mound-shaped brown wigwams - later I counted twenty. Like a chattering flock of geese, half-naked men, women, and children clad in animal skins gathered around me. Clutching my robe tightly, I endured their pointing, stares, and laughter. On the fringes of the crowd, dogs, their ribs sharp beneath scruffy gray fur, barked and bared their teeth. I fixed my eyes on the ground, sinking further and further into the folds of the robe. I wanted to shut out those dark faces peering into my own, the squawk of their voices booming and fading around me.

The crowd parted, and an old woman, hunched-back as a turtle, ambled toward me. With an abrupt wave of her hand, the voices and laughter ceased. Fighting terror, I peered from the robe's shadows. The old woman stared back at me. Her brown skin was crinkled with age, her nose sharply beaked. Thin gray braids lay like frayed ropes upon her shoulders.

The old woman placed a gnarled finger under my chin and gently raised my face to her own. "Ah, and what a pretty little Iroquois Wanaga has found for himself."

A man spoke. " Surely this child has run away. We must return her to Wanaga."

A woman called out. "Yes, to keep the girl will only bring the evil one's wrath."

Voice after voice joined in. "Return her." "What is an Iroquois child to us?" "Did the Iroquois take pity on my child? No, they killed her!" "And what of my husband, sent to the Hill of the Dead by an Iroquois war club?" "Yes, return the Iroquois pup to Wanaga! Let his vengeful spirit do what it will with her."

The old woman swiped angrily at the air. "Enough!"

The crowd silenced.

The woman squatted at my feet. Her hand for a moment touched the sneaker I wore on my good foot, fingered the hem of my jeans.

Her face clouded with puzzlement, but she quickly turned her attention to the injured foot.

"The child is hurt," the old woman said. "Nowuk, you will carry her to my wigwam."

She stood, her eyes slowly scanning the circle of faces as though daring someone to comment. The people avoided her eyes. Those nearest the old woman's wigwam stepped aside.

When I felt strong arms scoop me up from behind, I shut my eyes. I didn't want to see the dark faces close in again around me.

"Nowuk, lay the child on the mat here by the fire."

I felt the arms gently lay me down.

"Grandmother," Nowuk said, "I know you mean well, but Wanaga will be angry that you—"

"Say no more. The child stays in my wigwam, at least until she is healed. Ah, Nowuk, do you forget? I have dealt with that old crow, Wanaga, many times."

His face anxious, Nowuk averted his eyes from the old woman, gave a non-committal grunt and left the wigwam.

I felt the warmth of the fire, smelled the meat broth bubbling in the hearth pot. My mouth watered. I had forgotten how hungry I was. Cautiously, I opened one eye.

The old woman met my glance with a smile, warm and genuine, not the leering grimace of Wanaga. Her features seemed to lose their sharpness. Her eyes held a sparkle that was almost girlish. I responded with a nervous smile.

"Well, it seems you have a spark of life, after all," the old woman said and patted my hand. "Nemisa tells me you understand a little Akwanakai. That's good, for it certainly will make your life among us a little more bearable. Now, warm yourself with some soup, while I see to your injured ankle."

She turned to Nemisa, who squatted at her side. "Dish up the child some soup while I mix the herbs for a healing salve."

I hesitated when Nemisa held out the bowl. My fears about Wanaga's broth still ran through my mind.

Returning with the salve, the old woman knelt at my feet. "Take the soup, child. You will find I'm a far better cook than old Wanaga."

I pushed myself up to a sitting position, still clutching the robe around my shoulders, now more as a protective shield than for warmth. I used my other hand to take the bowl and cautiously sniffed. The soup smelled good. I took a sip, savoring the thick meat broth on my tongue. It had none of the bitter aftertaste of Wanaga's. I downed it in a few gulps.

With a pleased smile, the woman watched me finish the soup, then began to massage my ankle. Taking a small, shallow wooden bowl, she spit several times into it, sprinkled in a green powder, then stirred the mixture into a sticky paste with her finger. She chanted in a purring singsong that made my spine tingle. It reminded me of Wanaga's mutterings when he hunched over his amulets.

The woman glanced up. She squeezed my hand. "Child, there's no reason to fear."

With a gentle touch, she smeared the paste on my ankle, then bound it with a long strip of coarse-woven cloth. Already, I could feel the pain beginning to subside. My stomach was full, the fire warm. *Maybe, I'm safe here, after all.*

"Nemisa, bring me your extra skirt and leggings . We'll get the child into dry clothes."

The old woman made a move to remove the robe from my shoulders. I clutched it tighter, reluctant to part with my shield.

"Poor child." She made a clucking sound with her tongue. "Knowing Wanaga, he's probably been beating you. Slip off the robe, and I'll put some salve on those wounds, too."

I let her take the robe from my shoulders. The woman drew back with a gasp, her eyes wide with horror.

"What is it, Grandmother?" Nemisa asked. "Her strange clothing?"

The old woman licked her lips anxiously. "No, Nemisa, not her clothing. It's…it's that necklace." She fixed her eyes on me, her voice suddenly sharp. "That necklace. How did you come by it?"

I gulped, my hand instinctively gripping the pendant. "I… I…. " I felt a knot rise in my throat. What could I say? Even if they were able to understand my words, I could not deny I had stolen the necklace. And what horrible punishment might the Akwanakai reserve for thieves?

"But, Grandmother," Nemisa said, "she only understands Akwanakai. She can't speak, except in Iroquois."

"So it would seem." The old woman fingered my t-shirt, the hem of my jeans, then glanced again at the sneaker. She looked toward Nemisa. "These garments are not Iroquois. They are like none I have ever seen."

"Grandmother, surely they are made from cloth the Iroquois obtain from that strange tribe of the east, the men with white skin and ugly faces hairy as the bear's."

The old woman shook her head. "I have seen Iroquois wearing cloth from the White Men, but it was nothing like this. Even so, that necklace? When… how?" She extended her hand to touch it but stopped abruptly.

"Such a pretty shell," Nemisa said. "Look how the polished pearl of the pendant catches the firelight." She made a move to touch the pendant.

The old woman slapped her hand down. "Don't touch it, Nemisa! The necklace will burn anyone but its wearer."

Nemisa's eyes went wide. "It is magic, then?"

"Yes, strong, strong medicine. Only one person ever possessed that necklace, and she was lowered into her grave wearing it many winters ago. Sawahna, a great Akwanakai medicine woman. You have heard me speak of her as my mentor, for she was my teacher, as I now am yours."

"But, then how could the Iroquois girl get…." Nemisa's voice trailed off.

"Yes, how could she get the necklace…unless she stole it from Wanaga…which means he stole it from…." Her lips tightened into a hateful scowl. "That foul, despicable, old crow. Could he be so evil as to rob the dead?"

I spoke up, eager to incriminate Wanaga. "I know he stole the necklace. He even told me how he robbed the grave and—" I stopped when I saw them both staring blankly. Pulling my robe shield back over my shoulders, I sank into myself again. They didn't understand, and there was no possible way I could tell them.

The old woman's brow crinkled in puzzlement. "The words this girl speaks are not Iroquois." She turned to me. "Child, can you understand my words?"

I nodded.

"My name is Teepawn. What is your name?"

"It's Becca...and I'm NOT Iroquois." My lip trembled as I fought back the tears. "Matter of fact, I'm not even from this time. I came from...."

The old woman raised her finger to her lips. "Hush, child. I can understand nothing of such strange jabber. Now, listen carefully. I will place my hands, one on either side of your head and ask you a question. You will picture in your mind the answer. No words now, just pictures."

"But what if—"

"Shh...listen, child, listen. If you concentrate, block out all else but the picture in your head, perhaps I, too, will be able to see it and understand. But first I must see if I can make contact with your spirit. Now, close your eyes."

I complied.

Shutting her own eyes, Teepawn placed a hand on each of my temples and began to chant, her voice quavering up and down an alien scale. Suddenly, her eyes snapped wide open. Abruptly, she broke off her chant and drew back.

Nemisa put a hand on the old woman's shoulder. "Grandmother, are you all right? What is it?"

Teepawn's eyes misted over, and tenderly she took my hands in her own. "Sawahna, can it really be you, my beloved teacher and sister? But how? How can you and this child be one in spirit?"

My eyes jerked open. "No, not Sawahna! I'm Becca. Becca. BECCA MORRISON!"

The old woman gathered me close and rocked me until my sobbing eased.

"But, Grandmother," Nemisa whispered, "why did you call the Iroquois girl Sawahna?"

Teepawn glanced down at me, pressed my head tighter to her bosom, and whispered. "The child is Becca. Such she desires to be called, and we will honor her wishes, but somehow, deep within Becca's spirit is Sawahna as well. I heard her voice call out to me. Within this child, I sense her presence. How? Why? That I do not know."

The color drained from Nemisa's face. "The Iroquois is possessed by a ghost?"

"No, not a ghost. Sawahna had great power, far more than you or I shall ever have. But she used her power for good, not evil. Even in death, I cannot believe that she would reach from the grave and steal the body of one living. No, this child is not possessed. I sense rather a memory of things deep in her past, the way perhaps, Nemisa, your spirit memory retains a misty image of your mother, how lovingly she looked upon you the day of your birth and cuddled you to her breast even with her last breath. Somewhere, deep within your spirit, is that image, I am sure, yet you cannot bring it forth. So must memories hover in the shadows of my spirit, also. Who can say how far back such memories might go? To birth? The womb? Perhaps even to a time before." In a gesture of puzzlement, the old woman passed a hand over her eyes. "I do not understand, yet my heart tells me this is so."

"Is the girl, then, not an Iroquois?"

"Ah, Nemisa, such we must find out, if we are to protect her from Wanaga." The old woman stroked my cheek. "Listen, child, I must try again to understand the pictures inside your head. This time, I will speak only to the one you call Becca, summon only her memories. Do you consent?"

I gave an uneasy nod. As before, the woman placed her hands on my temples, and we both closed our eyes.

"Becca, I want you to picture the tribe you were born into, the faces of your mother, father, your kin, your wigwam."

Long moments passed. Teepawn, astonishment on her face, slowly dropped her hands to her sides.

Nemisa tugged on the long fringe of the old woman's sleeve. "Grandmother, what did you see?"

"So strange it was, I search for words. I...I saw a wigwam so huge, it was four, no, six men high. It was white with sharp edges, not rounded as our wigwams. I saw white faces with hair the color of dead leaves, a babe with hair as yellow as the sun, and a man with eyes the color of sky."

Ecstatic, I flung my arms around the old woman. "You understand. Finally, someone can understand!" I grabbed her hands and put them on my temples again. "Please, I want to tell you more."

Seeming to understand, she said, "Yes, Becca, yes. Remember, though, think in pictures. Your words have no meaning for me."

I nodded, impatient to get on with it.

"Now, tell me, child. How is it that you were captured and brought to the land of the Akwanakai?"

I concentrated on making a silent movie in my head. I pictured Gramma's kitchen, my hand snaking out to sneak fresh-baked cookies to share with Ben, my view of the Michigan countryside from my swing, Charlene, Ben...I screwed up my face with the effort of picturing Wanaga. I needed Teepawn to see the necklace around his withered neck, his hawk-nosed face, his black glittering crow eyes. There must be no mistake. She had to understand.

When I got to the part where Wanaga and I stood before the burial mound and watched Sawahna being lowered into her grave, the old woman gave a sharp gasp and lowered her hands. Tears misted her eyes. After a moment, she composed herself and we continued.

I re-lived in my mind the hunt through Gramma's house for Sawahna's bones, my return to the pines, and Wanaga kidnapping me to this time, this place. I pictured him in his wigwam, handing me the bowl of broth, falling into a deep sleep, then pictured my successful resistance to that last cup of broth, stealing the necklace from the peg, and everything that had occurred until I had entered the Akwanakai village.

"Well, that's all," I said, my voice trembling.

Teepawn cradled me in her arms. "You are safe now, Becca. I will not let Wanaga steal you again."

"Grandmother," Nemisa whispered, "is Becca an Iroquois?"

"No, Nemisa. That was Wanaga's lie."

"Then from what tribe does she come?"

"I struggle to explain, for I am not sure I even understand. Becca, I believe, comes from another time, many, many winters that are yet to come. She was born into a tribe of white-skinned Bear Faces... perhaps kin to those known now to the Iroquois. Wanaga through his evil medicine has somehow found a way to journey to that faraway time. I believe he sensed somehow in Becca the essence of Sawahna's spirit, just as I did. By kidnapping Becca, he sought to gain for himself the power Sawahna once possessed. And the necklace, I am sure of it, now, he must have—"

"She is mine!"

The wigwam flooded with sunlight as the animal skin covering the doorway was shoved aside. There Wanaga stood, a dark, looming shadow.

"My Iroquois slave," he roared. "I demand her immediate return!"

Teepawn shielded me with her body. "And is it the way of the Akwanakai to barge into an old widow woman's wigwam screaming like a madman?"

Wanaga let the door robe fall behind him. "You'll find I go where I please, Teepawn, when my purpose is to regain my property." His voice softened. "But, come now, let us not exchange unpleasant words. Nowuk told me you took the girl in to nurse her injured foot. For this act of charity, I thank you, Teepawn. But now I have come to claim my slave and will care for her injuries myself." He made a move toward the mat where I cowered in the shadows.

Teepawn stood, drawing herself up to her full height, crossed her arms over her chest. "The girl stays with me. I will give word to Nowuk that he shall provide you with a bear robe, a quiver of arrows, tobacco, and, upon the new harvest, four baskets of corn. Ayah, that is more than adequate payment for such a scrawny Iroquois girl-child."

Wanaga lowered his voice to a fierce hiss and slowly advanced. "Teepawn, you are bound by Akwanakai law to return my rightful property. The girl is mine. And I will take her NOW!"

But the old woman narrowed her eyes to slits and stood her ground. "Ah, and will you then lay hands upon me, also? For such, Wanaga, you will have to do to take back the child." She gave a snort of disgust when he drew back. "Dare you, of all people, speak to me of Akwanakai law? Is it the way of the Akwanakai to starve a child—be she enemy or not—tie her like a dog, then slowly bleed her of life with foul poisons? Do you think I cannot see the mark of your evil medicine upon her? Yes, Wanaga, I am bound to return to you your property and, if I do not, I am bound to make restitution to you for your loss. I have chosen the latter."

"Oppose me, Teepawn, and I will bring the matter before Okemaw and the council of clan leaders. I have every right to say she is no longer my slave, and therefore not an item of property for which you can barter. Instead I will declare her an escaped Iroquois captive and thereby demand her death. And such I will do, rather than allow you to keep the girl. Have no doubt they will see things my way. They have in the past and will again."

He gave an evil laugh. "Think, Teepawn. The council consists of warriors. They look to me for their war amulets. Do you really think they will sacrifice my good will for a worthless Iroquois child and a doddering old woman turned thief?"

"Wanaga, do you really think to frighten me as easily as you do the others with your acts of fierce bluster and idle threats? Do you forget, I also have power?"

His face twitched with rage. "So, 'idle threats,' is it? Well, we shall see! Before the sun sets on this day, you shall return my slave to me, or you shall watch the girl put to death. And no easy death for this one. No, the Rite of Blood Vengeance is what I will demand. Persist, Teepawn, and the ghosts of our slain women and children will dance tonight to the screams of the little Iroquois."

Wanaga spun on his heels and left.

With a loud groan, the old woman sank to the dirt floor and gathered me, trembling and sobbing into her arms.

"Grandmother," Nemisa whispered, "can he demand her death?"

"Oh, he will try, Nemisa."

"But you didn't tell him you know Sawahna's spirit is one with Becca's, that you know he stole the necklace. Surely then he would be afraid to go to the council."

"You're right, Nemisa. Then he would not approach the council. But he would become far more cautious, take the time to carefully weave his lies, to shape his evil medicine into a trap from which I fear Becca could never escape. But he remains ignorant of our knowledge and his ignorance shall be our strength."

As Teepawn cradled me in her arms her eyes took on a distant stare. She muttered into the flickering fire, "Wanaga, you play the fool so well. In such a rage you must have been to find Sawahna gone, you never stopped to notice she took back her necklace. And now you think yourself the spider, don't you?

Foolish old man. Scurry about in ever widening circles, back and forth, over and under. Spin your web, plotting all the while how you will trap your prey and suck her dry." A rasping chuckle escaped her. "Ah, no, Wanaga. It is you who shall flounder in the sticky, deadly strands of your own evil. And it is we who shall suck you dry."

SEVEN

Teepawn cast an anxious glance toward the doorway. "Quickly now, Becca, take off the leggings. The council will send someone to fetch us soon. None but Nowuk, Nemisa, and I have seen you dressed in those strange garments of your tribe, and so it must remain. If others see you wearing them, suspicions that Wanaga can use to his advantage are bound to arise."

My eyes shyly downcast, I stood, unzipped the jeans and let them fall to my ankles. I sniffed back tears as I handed over the last visible remnants of my twentieth-century life.

"Breechcloth, too," Teepawn said, as she folded the jeans and laid them on top of my filthy gray t-shirt.

I gave my head an emphatic shake, feeling the blood rise to my cheeks. "I'm not taking off my underpants!"

Teepawn had no trouble understanding the tone of my voice, the shake of my head, but brushed aside my objections with an abrupt swipe at the air. "No, off with it all. Your tribe's strange garments will only bring us bad luck." She wrinkled her nose. "Besides, they smell. No, far better you wear Nemisa's ceremonial garments."

Minutes later I stood before the hearth fire and brushed my fingers over the soft, velvety buckskin of the skirt, its long fringe dangling past my knees. The tunic, made of the same soft deerskin, hung to my hips, the sleeves deeply fringed, its bodice decorated with dyed porcupine quills in a rainbow pattern of zigzags and intertwining flowers. My hair was combed, glossed with bear oil, and braided into two thick braids that framed my face and hung halfway down my chest. On my feet were the old woman's moccasins.

She slipped the panther necklace over my head. "Always, child, you must wear this necklace. I believe now that it is truly yours. Sawahna has bequeathed it to you that you may have protection against Wanaga's evil medicine."

Teepawn stepped back and, cocking her head, looked me up and down critically. Her face crinkled into a smile. "Ah, yes, that is good. Now, Nemisa, bring me the rabbit skin robe. No, your old one is good enough, just something to cover her garments and conceal the necklace. Until the time is right, she must look as she did when first she entered the village." She placed the robe over my head and shoulders. "You must keep yourself covered, until I tell you to remove the robe. This is important. Do you understand?"

I gave a nod.

"You look Akwanakai, but that's not enough. You must act like one as well. An Akwanakai child does not look his elders in the eyes as you are continually doing. Such is bad manners and shows disrespect."

"But, I—"

She cut me off. "And, please, please, Becca, say no words, not even if the clan leaders directly ask you a question. The sounds you utter are so peculiar, like no language they have ever heard. Wanaga could easily use your speech to persuade them you are possessed by some evil-spirit manitou. And, if I am to convince them you are

Akwanakai, you must show no tears, make no outcry, not even if the death sentence is pronounced."

I swallowed hard and managed a nod.

She patted my hand. "And, if such happens, child, don't lose hope, because, even then, I have a plan that may still save you from death. Trust me. Only if the council judges you to be a coward will all be lost. And, take heart, we even have an ally in the council, my grandson Nowuk."

I swallowed hard, remembering Nowuk's visit to Wanaga that first day of my captivity. He seemed far more Wanaga's friend and ally than mine.

Teepawn caught the look of alarm on my face and said, "Have no fear, child. I know what you are thinking. But Nowuk has no more use than I for that old raven, Wanaga. He visits him only to obtain the amulets he must have for the warpath. In the making of war medicine, you see, Wanaga has no equal."

Cloaked in Nemisa's rabbit skin robe, my eyes carefully focused on the ground, I limped between Teepawn and Nemisa through the village. I tried not to wince, though pain stabbed my ankle with every step. "No tears, no outcry." The words kept ringing in my ears. I struggled to keep from shaking, to keep my eyes down so I didn't have to see all the cold stares. The crowd, silent and somber, parted before us. The old woman halted before the doorway of the largest wigwam.

She turned to Nemisa. "Perhaps, Granddaughter, it is best that you await us here." Then she called out, "It is I, Teepawn. We have come."

"Enter," was the deep-voiced response.

Nemisa, her eyes moist, gave my hand a farewell squeeze. Not trusting myself to respond to Nemisa's gesture without tears, I turned abruptly and followed Teepawn into the wigwam. *Maybe the old woman doesn't want Nemisa to come because then she'd have to watch me die*. My stomach tight with fear, I stood just inside the entrance and peered from the hood of my robe.

Six men were sitting cross-legged before the hearth, their faces and bare chests agleam with sweat and reflected firelight. As my eyes adjusted to the smoke-hazed murk, I began to see their features and immediately identified Wanaga. Wizened, sharp-nosed, he sat immobile, a statue carved of gnarled dark wood. I gave a shiver, glad I couldn't see the glint of his crow eyes.

Across from him sat Nowuk, the youngest of the men, tall and lean, his back straight as the trunk of a pine. I searched his face for reassurance that he was kind and would stick up for me, but his lips were sternly set, his eyes focused on the fire. The knot in my stomach tightened. My glance flew from one gaunt, dark face to another. All were grim, as though they had already decided my fate.

Teepawn and I stood rigid against the wigwam wall and I had the feeling we were invisible. No one spoke. In fact, no one had even glanced up when we entered. As I watched, Nowuk put to his lips a long-stemmed pipe, two eagle feathers dangling from its bowl. He inhaled deeply then, inclining his head, he ceremoniously presented it to the next man. In silence the pipe was slowly passed from man to man around the circle. The minutes dragged on.

I looked toward the old woman, trying desperately to catch her eye. Maybe, just maybe, the council had lost interest in this whole escaped captive business, after all. I watched another man take a long, drawn-out puff on the pipe.

Well, right now, they're sure more taken with their pipe smoking than with me. Seems the smartest thing might be to slip unnoticed out the door, then, maybe, they would just forget about the whole—

Abruptly, one of the men stood and turned to face us. He drew himself up to his full height. His face was stern, his cheekbones gleaming like copper doorknobs, his long hair streaked with gray. Like Wanaga, he wore a bear claw necklace. Scalp locks dangled like a long, thick-clumped black fringe from his belt.

"Teepawn, come forward," he said. "The council would speak with you."

She gave my hand a squeeze and whispered, "Stay here until I call you to my side."

Heart pounding, I flattened myself against the wigwam wall and watched her, head held high, walk toward the hearth and take her stand before the circle of men.

The man who was standing spoke, his voice cold and steady. "Teepawn, this man, Wanaga, has come to us with a serious grievance. He tells us that you have taken his slave into your wigwam, and that you refuse to return her."

"This is so, Okemaw. However, I offered him just payment for the loss of his property. Did he tell you this as well?"

Wanaga sprang to his feet. "I want no payments. I will have the girl!"

Okemaw spoke, "Teepawn, you well know Wanaga is within his rights."

"And do you attest also that it his right to cruelly abuse a child?" She slowly scanned the circle of men who carefully avoided her eyes. "Clan heads and noble warriors, I ask you, is it the way of the Akwanakai to torture a child? He has starved her, beaten her, tied her like a dog until the rope has eaten deep into the flesh of her ankle. He has used his foul potions to—"

"Okemaw," Wanaga cut her off, "is this council to concern itself with such trivial matters as how a man must deal with an unruly girl slave? Yes, it was necessary to tie her. What man could not see logic in that? If I had not, she would have run off that first night. And of course I gave her food, but only when she worked. The girl is a lazy Iroquois and, more often than not, refused to work. But, come, is the rearing of a girl-child an issue worthy for clan leaders to discuss in council?" His lips curled into a sneer as he fixed his eyes on Teepawn. "Perhaps, a better forum for such a discussion would be a council of women, rather than warriors." With that, he returned to sitting cross-legged before the fire, a smug grin on his face.

"Wanaga is right," Okemaw said. "A slave girl's treatment is not an appropriate issue for the council's consideration. No, we have convened here to decide a serious dispute that, if continued, will disrupt the harmony of the village." He leaned toward Teepawn and lowered his voice to a confidential whisper. "I do not intend to provoke Wanaga's wrath over such a matter as this. Think, Teepawn. The welfare of an Iroquois slave versus the welfare of the entire band? Surely you see my position, the necessity of returning the girl?"

The old woman's lips tightened to a straight line, her eyes seeking out Wanaga's. "No, the girl remains with me!"

"Teepawn, I warned you," Wanaga said. "It is you who have provoked me to this." He turned to Okemaw. "I hereby declare the girl an escaped Iroquois captive. By Akwanakai law, you must condemn her to death." His eyes glittered, his thin lips twitching with a desire to smile. "And I have the right to decide the manner of her death." He fixed his glare on me.

I melted against the wall, feeling the food that had been curdling in my stomach now begin to rise. With a mighty effort I swallowed down the sour liquid.

"I demand," Wanaga continued, "that the girl die in The Rite of Blood Vengeance and that the sentence be carried out immediately."

Nowuk rose. "I protest...not her death...." He glanced sadly toward his grandmother, as though asking her forgiveness. "I must concede that Wanaga has the right to demand it, but, my council brothers, such a manner of death? I know that I, for one, will not participate in the slow torture death of a child. The Rite of Blood Vengeance is a death reserved for an enemy warrior who dies with his battle song a challenge upon his lips. Such an enemy honors us with his courage. I ask you, my brothers, if we put to death this child in like manner, will you feel honor, or will you seek to hide your heads in shame?"

Wanaga snarled, "How dare you oppose me, Nowuk! I will have this girl put to death as I—"

Okemaw turned upon Wanaga. "No! With Nowuk, I agree. I will not condemn a child to die by The Rite of Vengeance. Be assured, Wanaga, on this I will not relent."

Wanaga responded with an angry snort. "Akwanakai law, has it no longer any meaning?"

Okemaw spoke, "I grant your right to demand her death. Execution shall be carried out immediately, as you requested, but it shall be done quickly and with mercy." His eyes took in the circle of men with the exception of Wanaga. "My brothers, are we agreed upon this?"

"Ayah, so it must be done."

"The girl must die."

"Ayah, but mercifully."

Around the circle, the men responded one after the other in the affirmative.

I held my breath as the men looked to the remaining man to speak. Surely Nowuk would defend me. He had to! I looked toward Teepawn, trying to catch her eye but she didn't even glance in my direction.

Nowuk rose slowly and spoke, his voice solemn, "Okemaw, I see no other way for this dispute to be resolved. I agree the harmony of the village must be preserved." He turned to his grandmother. "Perhaps, in time, you may come to see the girl's death as a kindness. It is either kill her or return her to Wanaga. Surely, you would not wish such a life upon the child?"

Panic pounded through my veins. *No, don't cry out. No tears.* I looked toward Teepawn. *OK, isn't it about time for your wonderful plan?* I chewed my lip to keep from crying. *But, what if she's decided Nowuk is right, that I'm better off dead?*

Okemaw spoke, his voice deep and somber. "The council rules that the Iroquois child shall die." He turned again toward the men. "Throat cut?" The men nodded in unison. "So it shall be. Teepawn, do you wish to leave before the sentence is carried out?"

"No, I will stay."

"So be it. Teepawn, call the girl forward."

I stifled a sob. My eyes darted toward the fur robe hanging across the doorway, then I remembered my injured ankle. Running would be impossible.

The old woman's eyes sought me out. "Come to me, child."

I flattened myself against the wall. How could I have been so stupid to believe that this old woman was going to help me? I swiped at the hot tears burning my cheeks. Teepawn extended her arm toward me, and our eyes met. In my mind, I heard her voice, "Trust me. Trust me, Becca." Over and over, and so clear it was as though the old woman had spoken, but her lips never once moved.

Focusing on her kindly face, I slowly approached the hearth fire. From the corner of my eye I saw a stocky, muscular man rise and stand at Okemaw's side. I took another step, then froze when I saw a blur of motion. The man had slipped something into Okemaw's hand. A knife? I felt a sob of terror rise in my throat.

"Becca, hear me," said a voice in my head, like the echo of a distant memory. "We must trust Teepawn. She will not let Okemaw kill us." But the voice was not Teepawn's. That voice—I remembered now—it was the same one I had heard singing through my own lips when I knelt in the pine needles and summoned Wanaga to the twentieth century. Beneath the robe, I grasped the panther pendant hanging warm against my chest. Raising my chin, I forced my feet to walk the last few paces to stand beside the old woman.

"Meesauk, hold the girl," said Okemaw.

The stocky man at Okemaw's side made a move toward me. In a gesture of gentle restraint, Teepawn placed her hand on the man's forearm and instantly he halted. His face perplexed, he looked toward Okemaw.

"Teepawn," Okemaw said, his voice severe, "step aside."

Her hand remained steady on Meesauk's forearm. "There is no need to forcibly restrain the child. Have you heard her cry out, beg for life? Has she not come forward to meet death with courage equal to any Akwanakai warrior? By virtue of her courage, Okemaw, I ask your patience. Stay your knife but one more moment and hear me out."

Wanaga sprang to his feet and shouted, "Can't you see the woman only seeks delay, a chance to soften your hearts toward the child. 'Akwanakai warrior' Teepawn calls her! Why the girl's no more than a sniveling, deceitful Iroquois brat. Give her the chance and, be sure, she will attempt escape again. Perhaps, next time though she won't be recaptured but, instead, lead Iroquois war scouts back to our village." Wanaga drew the hunting knife from his belt and advanced toward me. "Okemaw, if you haven't the stomach to slit the girl's throat, I do!"

Okemaw turned on him, his voice a fierce growl. "Wanaga, I advise you, remember well your place! Within this council, it is I who hold the power."

Wanaga nervously licked his lips and sank down on his bony rump. "Okemaw, please be assured, I meant no disrespect. Forgive me if I am overzealous in my concern for our ancient laws and the welfare of the band."

Okemaw gave a disdainful grunt and turned his attention to Teepawn. "Don't you see that you only add to the girl's anguish by prolonging this?"

"Hear me out, Okemaw. Then, if you still determine the child is to die, I ask only that you allow her to face the knife with dignity and honor, such that befits a daughter of the Akwanakai."

Okemaw raised his eyebrows. "'A daughter of the Akwanakai?' But we all know the girl is Iroquois."

"And so I thought also when I took her into my wigwam, until—" With a dramatic flourish Teepawn removed the robe from my shoulders.

"Sawahna's medicine necklace!" Okemaw's eyes went wide.

Wanaga pointed a gnarled finger at me. "Aiee! May all bear witness! The Iroquois has robbed the dead, dishonored the grave of a great medicine woman. All of you know Sawahna was buried with that necklace about her neck. Can there be any doubt in your minds now that this girl must be put to death?"

Teepawn took my trembling hand in her own. "Okemaw, you will find that the grass still grows undisturbed upon Sawahna's grave. This girl did not disturb the Hill of the Dead. No, she possesses this necklace because it was bequeathed to her by Sawahna herself."

The men responded with a communal gasp. Wanaga's face began to twitch with rage, his lips working horribly, shaping and reshaping silent curses he didn't dare say aloud.

"Sawahna bequeathed her necklace to this Iroquois?" Okemaw asked. "These are strange words indeed, Teepawn."

"So it must seem, Okemaw. Yet, hasn't it happened before that a kindly spirit has bequeathed upon the living the means to survive?" She turned to a man with long white hair. "Muqua, was it not, when you were a young man and lost in a blizzard, that the spirit of your father appeared to you in a dream. He led you to a snow-covered cache and there you found food, robes, and shelter. The spirit of your father gave you the means to preserve your life. Is this not so?"

Muqua assented with a nod. "Ayah, I do know that is true. To my dead father's spirit, I owe my life."

Teepawn put her arm around my shoulders. "So also the spirit of Sawahna has given us a sign in this, her medicine necklace. She asks that we spare this child, take her among us to live out her life as an adopted daughter of the Akwanakai. This I truly believe."

Wanaga spoke out. "Aiee, I feel evil. **Evil**." He drew out the word a second time in a long eerie trill. "This girl. She is possessed by the dead. Leave us, spirit," he moaned, his eyes rolling vacantly in their sockets. "Be gone, Evil Demon. Evil Manitou! Ghost return to your grave."

He gave a start and shook his head abruptly as though breaking free from some horror that had temporarily seized him. "Okemaw, I... I tried, but not even I can drive from her the evil demon. We must immediately cast the Iroquois from the village. I fear her presence here will bring plague and starvation down upon us all."

Teepawn gave a snort of disgust and turned to Okemaw. "Can you now understand why I waited until the death sentence was pronounced? I was holding out, hoping other reasons would cause the council to spare the child." She jerked her head in Wanaga's direction. "I knew he would claim the child possessed by a ghost the moment I spoke of Sawahna's spirit intervening to save her. You all know how Wanaga hated Sawahna in life, saw her as a rival for his power. Would he not seek to destroy the child Sawahna has chosen to succeed her?"

Wanaga's lip curled back in a vicious snarl. "You doddering old hag! Dare you accuse me of such deceit? Okemaw, there is evil in this wigwam. I feel strongly its presence. Though I was wrong about the Iroquois as its source. I sense now the evil resides not in the girl but rather in you, Teepawn."

Nowuk lunged for Wanaga. "You've no right to speak so!"

Okemaw put his hand firmly on Nowuk's shoulder, his voice stern. "Lay no hand on him. Remember, Nowuk, you are a man chosen for the council and must show restraint." He turned to Wanaga. "My brother, know you that your war medicine is revered by our warriors. Know also, though, that this woman, Teepawn, is equally revered for her healing powers. If you have an accusation, speak it out clearly, so that she may answer to it."

Wanaga's black eyes glittered as he spoke. "Think, my council brothers, why would a great Akwanakai medicine woman, such as Sawahna, single out an Iroquois as her successor? Why would she reach beyond the grave and bestow upon an enemy child her sacred medicine necklace?" He fixed his eyes on Teepawn. "No, I contend the old woman only pretended to put that necklace upon Sawahna when she wrapped her corpse for the grave. We have only Teepawn's word that Sawahna was buried with the necklace. I say all along she kept it for herself. And now we see for what evil purpose. In the Iroquois girl she has found one she can manipulate and, through her, Teepawn seeks to usurp Sawahna's medicine power and prestige."

Teepawn sputtered out a laugh. "So, now it is I who stole the necklace? I advise you, be careful of your accusations, Wanaga. Remember, robbing the dead carries with it the sentence of slow death by torture." She faced Okemaw. "If it was my purpose to possess the necklace you know I could have done so at Sawahna's death. All accepted me as Sawahna's successor. None would have questioned my right to possess her medicine necklace. No, it was I who decided Sawahna should be buried with it upon her neck. Though, maybe, Okemaw, you are right to question where the girl got the necklace. Perhaps," her eyes sought out Wanaga's in the shadows. "just perhaps, there is another explanation. If the girl did not rob the Hill of the Dead, that does not eliminate the possibility that ten winters ago, when Sawahna was laid in her grave, someone else...."

Wanaga, his face dripping with sweat, spoke up, his voice unsteady. "I... I will accept Teepawn's answer to my accusation." His eyes darted nervously toward Teepawn then looked quickly toward Okemaw.

"Forgive an old man's lack of tact. My concern is always first for the safety of the band." He chewed his lip and added quickly, "Iroquois scouts, you know. Well, perhaps the girl would be less likely to run if cared for by a woman. And, also, that puny, crippled girl Nemisa can be of little help to Teepawn in her old age. She needs someone, like the Iroquois, whole in body and strong. I...uh, well, I...."

He drew a deep breath, as though it took great effort to force the words from his mouth. "I relinquish my claim to the girl."

EIGHT

Days melted into weeks. With Teepawn and Nemisa's patient tutoring, I quickly learned to speak Akwanakai. The soft flowing sounds and the rhythm of its phrases often echoed in my mind with a strange familiarity as though I were remembering the words rather than learning them for the first time.

The villagers had accepted Teepawn's explanation that Sawahna's spirit had intervened to save me, which helped to wipe away my stigma as a captive Iroquois. Wanaga had disappeared from his wigwam and hadn't been seen since the night the council met to decide my fate. I hoped he was gone forever, but Teepawn assured me he wasn't. "No, child, like pain and pestilence, that evil old raven always returns." His comings and goings had always been a mystery to the band. He was in the habit of disappearing for moons at a time and then, without warning, reappearing.

I wondered if he was back in the twentieth century, lurking around, trying to lure some other poor kid into his web? Ben? Maybe Charlene? My face twitched with a smile but then grew solemn. No, I wouldn't wish such a fate on anyone, not even Charlene Boersma.

* * *

One evening I joined a group of the women who sat cross-legged around the wigwam fire. With a bone awl and deer sinew, I sewed the last laborious stitches on my first pair of moccasins. I had embroidered them carefully with rainbow arches of porcupine quills.

"Grandmother," —for that is how I had come to think of Teepawn, the woman who had rescued me and shown me so much care and love— "I made these for you, to thank you for taking me into your home."

She responded with an embrace and warm praise for my needlework. The next day, after watching her hobbling about, I hesitantly asked if perhaps they weren't too small. She heartily insisted, no, the moccasins were the finest of gifts, but decided, after another day of painful hobbling, that it might be prudent to save such a fine gift for ceremonial occasions only.

In the early moons of spring I helped the women and children plant the fields with corn, beans, and squash. Later, using a stick with a large clamshell bound to its tip, I hoed the weeds from around the tender young corn and bean shoots. Then, as the cool days of spring lengthened into early summer, I followed Grandmother on her daily excursions into the forest to search for healing herbs and the edible roots that grew wild. I learned the names of the plants, their uses, how to find them, and carried a burden basket on my back in which to collect them. The forest became my classroom, Grandmother my teacher.

"Listen, Becca," Grandmother would say, "do you hear? It is the song of Oophanqua, the oriole. He is calling to his little wife, and there, child, hear how sweetly she answers him." Grandmother taught me to identify each bird by its song, but cautioned me, "Beware the call of the whip-poor-will. It can be not a bird at all but the call of one Iroquois scout to another. So also, Becca, the call of the owl, especially when the moon is high."

Grandmother showed me the location of each of the family's four food caches. Each family possessed several, hidden throughout the forest. The large pits were lined with bark to make them watertight and to insure their walls of sandy soil wouldn't collapse. The entrance to each cache was camouflaged with a grid of saplings interwoven with soil, living grass and plants, making its location almost impossible to detect. Not only were the caches used to store food for the winter moons, but the empty ones made ideal hiding places for the women and children in case of attack. Again and again, I had to find each cache until Grandmother was satisfied I could locate their hidden entrances without fail.

I learned to read animal tracks and even their droppings, to tell the animal's species, age, whether it was male or female, and how long it had been since it had passed that way.

Nothing escaped Grandmother's notice. Taking my hand, she led me to a tree. "What do you see, child?" she asked.

"Long white strips torn in the bark."

"See the pattern of the stripes." She took my hand and brushed my fingers over the wounds in the tree trunk. "And feel the depth of the gashes. Remember, Becca, what you feel and see, for this is the sign of Mukcenuk, the grizzly bear." Grandmother brushed a clump of ferns to one side. "See, here are the tracks. Tell me, what do they say?"

I sat on my haunches and carefully examined the footprints. "The bear has a little one, a cub."

"Ah, good." Grandmother narrowed her eyes, her voice intense. "Nothing, Becca, nothing, not even an Iroquois, is more dangerous than a she-grizzly with a cub."

She taught me to use not only my sight and hearing, but even taste and smell to know the forest and read the signs of the animal tribes that lived there.

"Smell the air, Becca. Tell me, what animal passed here only a short time ago?"

I obediently sniffed the air and, after a little thought, ventured, "Cawshu, the bobcat?"

Grandmother's face crinkled into a smile. "Ayah, you remembered. Is good. Now, Becca, take a leaf from each of these two plants. They look the same, don't they? But taste them—a good medicine woman knows the plant with the bitter leaves is far better for healing a wound."

After each morning's excursion in the forest, Grandmother and I would return to the wigwam where Nemisa met us with a hug and a cup of broth. Placing the contents of my burden basket in her lap, Grandmother would settle down before the hearth to sort through what we had gathered, separating the roots for the evening's stew from the healing herbs she would later use to make her medicines. Nemisa and I would sit beside her, waiting for the old woman to begin the last part of the day's lesson, the questions and, if we were lucky, maybe a story or two before she shooed us out to play.

One day, Grandmother laid out three sprigs of leaves on the hard dirt floor. "Nemisa, a woman brings to you her child. He cries with a pain in the belly. You touch his abdomen, and it is as though he has swallowed a rock. What do you do?"

Nemisa pointed to a feathery sprig of leaves. "I would give him a tea made from the boiled leaves of the Ahawa fern."

With a warm smile, Grandmother nodded and turned her attention to me.

"Now, Becca, think back to this morning, when we walked the forest path. On which side of the tree is the bark a lighter color?"

My face fell. "But I never thought to look."

Frowning, Grandmother slowly shook her head. "Ah, Becca, an Akwanakai medicine woman must always 'think to look.' She must learn to walk in silence, her ears and eyes open to the wisdom the forest teaches. Ayah, too often I see you walk to the tune of your own chatter. Tomorrow you will look for the answer to this question."

I felt my cheeks color. Though she was always gentle, I knew when Grandmother was disappointed and vowed that the next day she would be proud of me.

When the days began to grow hot, and the corn had reached the height of a man's shoulder, Grandmother commissioned a herald to announce a feast. The man, carrying the invitations in the form of small bundles of tobacco, went from wigwam to wigwam, leaving one for each family and crying out as he walked, "Hear, oh clansmen and friends! The medicine woman, Teepawn, announces a great feast to celebrate the adoption of her new granddaughter."

As I listened to the man call out the invitation I wanted to hold my ears and block out his words. Though I loved Teepawn and called her Grandmother, being officially adopted into the Akwanakai tribe slammed a door on my life as an American girl and the family I loved so very much. Christmas, my birthday, my family gathering around the TV with a bowl of popcorn, even listening to the Beatles on my new transistor radio with my best friend Judy. All were gone. No, not gone, but none of that would exist until three hundred or four hundred years in the future. A more disturbing thought was that I might never even exist in that time. How could my family and friends even miss someone they never knew? I shook my head to banish the thought, but I knew the future would always haunt me. I had no choice after all. Here I was. I had Teepawn, Nemisa, a family who loved me. I knew I should be grateful. Things could have been much worse. I looked around me and, seeing my Akwanakai family preparing for my adoption ceremony, my dark cloud lifted.

Throughout the many days of feast preparations, Nowuk's wife, Chumeka, worked at Grandmother's side. She was a young woman, her eyes wide and gentle as a doe's, her body slender as a girl's. While her first-born son gurgled happily in his cradleboard and swayed from a tree branch, Chumeka and Grandmother dug basket after basket of potatoes and turnips for the feast. As the feast day drew nearer, other clanswomen joined the two women to help butcher the deer and rabbits Nowuk had provided and to slice the endless baskets of vegetables for the stew. Nemisa and I searched the forest for the bushes that grew the juiciest ripe berries and returned again and again to fill our burden baskets.

Gifts that Grandmother and Chumeka had been making for two moons mounded against the wigwam wall into a hill of moccasins, baskets, cloth bags woven of milkweed fibers, shell jewelry, and, for the children, a basket heaped with maple sugar candies. Nemisa and I made the candy using carved wooden molds. We pressed the maple sugar into four different indentations then, when we pried it out, the candies were in the crude shapes of a bear, a fox, a fish, or a bird. Nowuk provided the fur robes, quivers of arrows, and flint axes Grandmother would give to her guests.

Thinking of all my birthday parties back home in the twentieth century, it struck me what an opposite view the Akwanakai took of a party. They would have been horrified to hear of a host or hostess who expected a guest to bring a gift. Here, it was always the guest who received the gift.

The day of the feast arrived and, true to her word, Grandmother brought out the moccasins I had made and hobbled about in them throughout the two days' festivities. I wore my glossy black hair bound into two braids, each woven through with an otter tail. An eagle feather dangled by each cheek. Grandmother painted my face with streaks of red ochre. The panther necklace rested upon the bodice of the embroidered buckskin shirt she had made for me, her new granddaughter.

When Grandmother sang a chant of thanksgiving to the Great Manitou and made an offering to the Four Directions with tobacco which she sprinkled over the fire, I was formally welcomed into the Akwanakai tribe. After two days of dancing, games, and feasting on venison stew with new potatoes and turnips, the wild rice manoomin, combined with maple syrup, and berries and maple sugar candy, the guests finally returned to their own wigwams. Life settled again into the routine I was beginning to accept as my new life.

* * *

I awoke to Nemisa's scream. "Sister, wake up, quick! They're attacking again."

Grabbing my weapon—two pieces of split deadwood—I sprang to my feet with a shrieking war whoop and over and over banged the wood planks together. On the opposite side of the same six-foot-high wood platform, Nemisa, my fellow warrior, was screaming and frantically waving a long strip of red cloth.

During the late summer when the corn, beans, and squash were nearly ready for harvest, the village girls took turns being human scarecrows. Five platforms were positioned at strategic points throughout the fields, and a team of two sat atop each one. Our time on duty generally amounted to a couple hours a day for each girl. But half of the girls had recently left with their families, bound for a campsite where the Akwanakai went each summer to trade with the Hurons. The girls whose families had remained behind to tend the crops had to double their allotted time on the platforms. To help pass the long, boring hours, Nemisa and I devised the warrior game. Our enemy, a flock of twenty-some black birds, took flight with a raucous communal squawk and a clattering rush of wings. One, a little braver than the rest, settled back down to feast on a nearly ripe ear of corn.

Nemisa pointed toward him. "Becca, over there."

I stooped and chose a small round pebble from the mound of stones I had piled on the platform. I hefted it, blew on it for good luck, then rearing back my arm, heaved it at the bird. The pebble whizzed through the air. With a loud squawk, the enemy warrior soared into the air, a lone black feather fluttering to the ground in his wake.

I gave a shrill whoop. "Well, what do you think, Nemisa? Did I get that old bird or not?"

Nemisa giggled. "Ayah, such a fearless fighter you have become. You counted coup on him for sure. Tonight, around the fire, the warriors will sing your praises."

"What does 'counted coup' mean?" I asked, my eyebrows raised in a question at the unfamiliar words.

"Oh, it means you touched an enemy with your weapon. Our people believe a warrior need not necessarily kill an enemy. It is enough to merely touch him and then escape without injury. You may not think it, but riding into an enemy camp and landing a blow on an enemy warrior and then escaping can take more courage and skill then killing him. A dead warrior can't respect your courage and skill. A live one must do so and try to avenge his humiliation."

With a hearty laugh, I settled back down on the platform, pillowing my head on my arms. "Want me to take over the watch yet, Nemisa? After all, I've now counted coup!"

Nemisa shook her head. "No, mighty warrior, I'll take my full turn." Shading her eyes, she checked the angle of the sun. "Shouldn't be that long, anyway, until Aneesay and Nanowe come to relieve us."

Hoping to resume my dream, I closed my eyes. I'd been dreaming of home, Mama and Daddy. Gramma and Grampa came to visit for Christmas. We'd been decorating the tree, but instead of the shiny balls, colored lights, and tinsel which the others were putting on the tree, I'd tied an eagle feather to each branch.

Sleep wouldn't return. I lay listening to the lazy humming of the bees, the sharp clatter of the grasshoppers. From the forest I heard the distant song of the thrush calling to her mate. I fought the tears that burned my eyelids. The villagers were kind. I had friends among the children. Grandmother, Nemisa, Nowuk, and Chumeka all loved me. I told myself I should be happy. Still, the tears burned.

So much…I missed Mama, Daddy, Gramma and Grampa, even little baby Terry. So much. Babies grew so fast. Would he even know me anymore? And what about Mama and Daddy? Would they forget they ever had a skinny girl with coke bottle glasses and stringy light-brown hair who liked to play Indian? I struggled to bring to my mind, one by one, the faces of my twentieth-century family. I was terrified that their features, which I now could summon so vividly, would with time blur and finally be lost to me forever.

NINE

Nemisa and I paused beside the long, open meadow that served as the village game field. With gusto, I threw myself into the squealing, cheering group of girls and young children who were watching the boys play stickball. The game's excitement, the noise, the camaraderie always helped me forget how homesick I was.

Occasionally, when the teams were unevenly matched, the boys would condescend to letting a girl or two join their game to even the sides. I had played a few times on those terms and found I loved the game. My twentieth-century body had been tall, awkward and gangly, totally inept at catching a ball. But the body I now found myself occupying was fast, wiry, and agile. Sports were fun now, instead of the embarrassing ordeal they had once been. With half the boys gone from the village, I figured there was a good chance short-handed teams would let a girl join the game. If that happened today, I intended to be that girl.

Nemisa stood shyly apart. "Becca," she called. "Remember we promised Grandmother we would gather a basket of nuts before we returned to the wigwam."

I gestured toward the sun. "Oh, come on, Nemisa. We have over half a day left. Let's stay a while and watch."

She gave a helpless shrug and sat forlornly on the ground, a safe distance from the field, so she wouldn't be trampled by an over-exuberant player giving chase to the ball.

My face grew solemn as I watched Nemisa and remembered my own pain of often being left out. I glanced back at the game, then again at Nemisa and vowed to myself, I won't play long, just a little while.

Nemisa flashed me a smile that said, Aw, Becca, go ahead and have fun. I'll be OK.

At both ends of the playing field, a goalpost, a man and a half high, had been erected. Each player was armed with a stick, its end looped into a small racket and its grid woven of sinew. The object was to get the ball made of a wad of deer hair bound with sinew to hit the top of the opposing team's goalpost. A player could use either his hands or racket to propel the ball. Charging, blocking, wrestling, clawing—whatever it took to gain the ball from an opponent—was permitted.

Tense with excitement, I watched the knotted tangle of flailing bronze limbs and stick rackets. The ball shot through the air, and a boy leapt from the squirming pile of bodies like a deer from the underbrush. He pounced on the ball, rolled over and sprang to his feet in one fluid motion. Shrieking his war whoop, he ran toward the goal with the rest in pursuit. Looking over his shoulder, he saw two boys gaining on him. With a mighty fling of his racket, the ball soared toward the goalpost just before the boys crashed into him.

A cheer went up from the girls as the ball hit the goal.

"Quawno, he scores again!" yelled one.

"Just watch," said one of the older girls, "the men will ask him to play with them at the Harvest Feast games."

"Aiee! Listen to Meenaka. She sings the praises of her lover."

The older girl's cheeks colored deeply. "Why, such nonsense you speak! Quawno is only a boy, fourteen winters, not even a warrior yet."

Quawno scrambled free of the pileup. He stood lean and straight, with a white-toothed grin. His grin disappeared when he realized that the girls were watching him. It was replaced by the serious face a man should always show in victory. But, as his teammates clamored noisily over him, the grin won out. Two younger boys were stumbling toward the sidelines, one limping, the other holding his hand over a nose that was gushing blood.

I fought the urge to rush to them and offer help. I had done just that the first time I watched a game, only to be angrily rebuffed. The boys, even the littlest, considered themselves stickball warriors. A girl sympathetically fawning over their injuries was an insult. Like the other girls, I politely averted my eyes from the two injured mini-warriors.

Quawno and the leader of the other team met in the center of the field. After a few moments of discussion, Quawno called out to the girls, "Is there one among you who will play? We have lost two to the enemy."

The older girls tittered and began to push Meenaka, loudly protesting, toward the playing field.

I called out, "I'll play."

When Quawno gave a nod, I hiked my skirt above my knees, tied it with my sash and grabbed a stick from the pile of extras, then ran for the center of the field. I flexed my knees into a crouch and waited for the toss. Four of the biggest boys, Quawno among them, stood at the center in a face-off. Another boy approached, paused with his head upturned like a cock about to crow then, uttering an ear-shattering shriek, threw up the small black ball.

Lost for a moment in the glare of the sun, the ball finally came back into sight. In a crescendo of yells, cheers, and war whoops, everyone tried to catch it in mid-air but bumped into each other. I scrambled clear of the pileup in time to see the ball scooped up, sail past my ear, and roll into the high grass at the field's edge. I ran, pounced upon it, and looked up to see a boy charging right for me.

"Quick, over here!" Quawno shouted.

I flung the ball blindly in the direction of his voice and tensed for the collision. When none came, I was back on my feet running after the retreating cloud of dust. Back and forth, from one end of the field to the other, we ran, until my sides ached and my breath came in gasps. The teams were evenly matched and the score stayed close.

Then it was the last round, and we all waited tensely for the toss-up. When it came, Quawno outran the crowd and it seemed certain that he would net the ball. But another boy threw himself at Quawno's feet and tripped him. The rest of the boys piled on the two of them in a furious tangle of limbs and sticks. I took a position on the outskirts, to scoop up the ball if it surfaced.

Suddenly, it dribbled out of the writhing mass of bodies. Like a cat, I pounced on it and, with cheers ringing in my ears, was off and running for the goalpost. I heard a runner coming up fast behind me and, gauging the distance to the goalpost, decided to try to fling the ball. It only took an instant for me to place the ball in my racket and rear my arm back for the fling, but the runner caught up with me, grabbed me around the waist and threw me to the ground.

I lay for a moment, my head spinning with the force of the impact, the other runners leaping over my body with no more concern than a herd of deer jumping over a boulder in their path. I tentatively touched the scrape on my forehead, then swiped at the blood dripping into my eyes. With a groan, I pushed myself to a sitting position. The world was still spinning as I shakily stood up. A cheer went up for the opposing team. Mine had lost.

I fought back pain as I dejectedly headed for the sidelines. I knew it would be shameful to acknowledge my pain publicly. Hearing someone behind me, I looked over my shoulder. My pain was forgotten It was Quawno.

"May I walk with you?" he asked.

I swallowed hard and gave a nod. "I'm sorry. Guess if it weren't for me, our team might have won."

"No, you should not be ashamed. In fact, you played as well as any boy. That is what I wanted to tell you. Ayah, never have I seen a girl run so fast."

I wanted to give out a joyous yelp but settled for a smile and an appropriately demure "Thank you." Quawno, spotting the tittering older girls on the sideline, faded into the crowd of boys as quickly as he had appeared. With my head held high, I graciously accepted the girls' congratulations and Meeneka's envious glances, then went off to find Nemisa.

I found her sitting beneath a maple tree. At her feet sat a circle of young children, their round-cheeked faces rapt with attention. I sat down nearby to listen as Nemisa finished her story.

"And as the buck leapt into the clearing, the maiden called out to her grandfather to stay his arrow. But, alas, she heard the twang of his bow and knew she was too late. The buck crumpled to his knees, for the arrow had run true and pierced his heart. With the buck's death, the spell of the evil sorcerer was broken and, in a puddle of blood lay, not the body of the deer, but her warrior lover. She cried out to The Great Manitou and he took pity upon her. To this day, if you look upon the sky on a clear night, you will see among the stars the form of that mighty stag and his doe, for the Great Manitou decreed, "Never again shall the two lovers be separated."

"Another story, Nemisa!"

"Ayah, please, tell one more!"

Catching sight of me, Nemisa told the children, "I'm sorry. No more stories today. Maybe tomorrow."

At my insistence we stopped at the stream before looking for a tree ripe with nuts. We left our skirts on the sandy bank and plunged into the icy water. In the water, Nemisa was free of her handicaps. We cavorted and splashed like a pair of otters, then emerged to lie on the moss-covered bank. While a whip-poor-will sang his song on the breeze, we dozed in the sun.

Nemisa awoke first and gently shook my shoulder. "Hey, sister," she laughed, "you'll sleep the day away."

I yawned and stretched. "Oh, let's not go just yet. Hey, how about if I teach you some more word pictures?"

Nemisa responded with an eager nod. I had been teaching her how to read and write. Using a stick, I would spell Akwanakai words in the dirt—as best I could phonetically—then translate them into English. It was an intriguing game to Nemisa, and, for me, a tie to my former life. I chose a sharp stick and scraped away the leaves and moss, so I had a smooth place to write.

"OK, what'll it be today?" I asked Nemisa.

She pondered, then said, "Let's practice the pictures for names again."

I etched into the sandy dirt, "Nemisa."

Nemisa smiled. "My name picture?"

I nodded. "Now, let's see if you can read it in English." I wrote, "Singing Bird."

An eager student, Nemisa insisted on erasing the letters and painstakingly forming each letter for herself. After she'd mastered her name, I showed her Teepawn and translated it into the English version, "Speaks with Wolves." Nemisa wanted to learn the names for each member of our family, Nowuk or "Stands Tall," Chumeka or "Star Dawn," and their baby, Oocha or "Chipmunk."

As Nemisa labored with the "k" in Chipmunk, I glanced toward the sun sinking low in the west. "Nemisa, I guess we ought to be hunting for that nut tree."

Her brow furrowed with concentration, she gave a disinterested shrug. "Ah, I spotted a muskrat den in the creek bank, while we were swimming. We can look for the nut tree tomorrow and borrow roots from the muskrat today."

"What do you mean 'borrow' from the muskrat?"

Nemisa erased her clumsy attempt at a "k" and began again. "Oh, the muskrat stores all sorts of good-tasting roots in her den for winter. All we have to do is dig into the stream bank, and we'll have enough roots to fill both our burden baskets."

I thought a moment. "But what about the poor muskrat? If we steal her food, won't she starve to death in the winter?"

"Oh, we won't take it all. Why, we could never carry even one-half of her stores, if we had four baskets. Don't worry, she'll have plenty left for herself and her young ones, too."

A chorus of unearthly yowls and shrieks pierced the air.

Her eyes wide with fear, Nemisa held herself rigid. "The war cry of the Iroquois," she whispered, as though it were too awful a thing to say aloud.

I sprang to my feet and looked in the direction of the village. Heavy black columns of smoke were mushrooming above the trees.

I extended my hand to Nemisa and pulled her to her feet. "Can you make it to the nearest food cache?"

Nemisa nodded. "But what about you?" she called after me. I had already taken off at a run down the path that led to the village. "Where are you going?"

"To look for Grandmother," I called over my shoulder.

I heard Nemisa shouting something, but her words were lost, dissolving among the distant shrieks and the loud resounding crack of firearms. As I ran, I thought of Grandmother's slow, hobbling gait. *Were the lookouts able to give an early enough warning? Perhaps the Iroquois will spare an old woman.* Then I remembered Nowuk's stories of past Iroquois massacres and ran faster.

I heard a mother's high-pitched scream for her child and my skin prickled. At the sound of fast approaching footsteps, I dove into the underbrush and peered between the leaves. Women carrying bundles, some with cradleboards strapped to their backs, or dragging young children by the hand, ran by my hiding place. Terror distorted the familiar faces.

I stood and called out to one of the women, "Waweema, have you seen Teepawn?"

The woman shook her head and broke into loud sobs. "My son—only four winters and they...they...."A gray-haired woman grabbed her hand and gently pulled her forward. "Come, Waweema, your death will not bring your son back." She looked toward me. "Run, child! Save yourself!"

I smothered a sob and darted back onto the path. The smell of smoke choked the air as I neared the village. Hearing more footsteps, I stepped behind a tree. Chumeka, her baby on her back and Grandmother clinging to her arm, appeared around the twist in the trail.

"Grandmother," I yelled, rushing toward the old woman. "Chumeka, run ahead with your baby. I'm here to care for Grandmother now."

Chumeka hesitated.

Grandmother pushed both of us away. "No, you run. I'm an old woman. I'll only slow you. I've lived long enough."

From several twists back on the trail came a shrieking yowl.

Grandmother jerked my hands from her arm. "Run, my granddaughters! RUN!"

Tears streaming down her face, Chumeka kissed Grandmother's cheek and ran down the path.

Fire sparking her eyes, Grandmother turned on me. "You will obey me! Now RUN! Let me at least die knowing my granddaughters will live."

The yowl sounded again. I gave Grandmother a hug, then followed Chumeka at a run. When I was out of the old woman's sight, I darted into the thick underbrush. After Grandmother had hobbled by, my heart began to pound so loud I was certain the Iroquois would hear it long before he passed my hiding place. I sifted through the sandy soil at my feet, until I found two small round pebbles. Clutching them, one in each palm, I waited. A mosquito lit on my nose, but I didn't dare move a muscle to dislodge it. It gorged itself in peace, as sweat dripped in rivulets down my cheeks.

Then I heard it, the fast approaching cushioned rhythmic slap of moccasins. I held my breath as the Iroquois turned the twist in the trail and passed me at a fast trot. His face was a grotesque mask of black and red paint, his hair shaved except for a brush-like strip that ran down the center of his head, from his forehead to the nape of his neck. In his hand he carried a viciously spiked war club stained red with blood. I saw the three bloody hanks of hair dangling from his belt and vowed he wouldn't add Grandmother's to his grisly collection.

Peering from between the branches, I waited until I saw him nearing the far twist of the trail. Swallowing the knot of terror in my throat, I slowly stood.

"Hey, broom-head," I called out in English. He stopped short and spun toward my voice. "Yeah, that's right, you with the moldy, black scrub brush on your head!" I drew my arm back and heaved first one pebble then the other, with all the power I could muster. Both hit their marks, his cheek and shoulder.

His lips curled into a ferocious snarl. Raising his war club, he gave a piercing shriek and lunged toward me. I dove back into the underbrush and wormed my way under bushes. In order to pursue me, he had to claw his way through their branches. Twice, he lost me in the thick cover and I was able to lengthen the distance between us. My goal had been to lead him away from Grandmother. That accomplished, I now had to save my own life. Far away, I heard him crashing through the bushes in search of me and figured I could now safely make my way back to a trail. There I hoped to get my bearings and search out a food cache.

Thorns clawing my face and clothes, I inched my way toward the path far to the west of where the Iroquois was still thrashing through the bushes. I reached the path and sprang to my feet. With Grandmother's training hammered into me, I instantly knew where to go and broke into a run. I had only a few more yards to run when I heard his footsteps coming up fast behind me. I dove back into the bushes and crawled toward the big oak tree. I felt frantically among the gnarled roots for the knob of the entrance cover and pulled, but it wouldn't budge. I stood and gave the cover a mighty yank. Finally, the tangle of grass roots gave way, and I was able to lift the cover. Jumping into the dank hole, I pulled the cover over me and felt as if I was closing the lid of my own coffin.

Panic pounded a steady beat in my head. I knew I hadn't camouflaged the cover the way Grandmother had taught me. There was no way, I told myself, the Iroquois wouldn't see the upturned roots of grass, the clumps of loose soil.

Crouching in a tense knot, I heard his footsteps pound, causing soil to tumble around me. I held my breath, until the footsteps faded and, at last, were gone. Minutes melted into more minutes. When I had begun to feel that maybe I would keep my hair after all, I heard the footsteps again... slow, deliberate this time. I knew then that he was backtracking. It was only a matter of time before he found me.

A muffled war cry came to my ears, this time Akwanakai. I prayed the band's warriors had regrouped and were making a counter offensive. I heard the voices of two men speaking Iroquois, arguing from the sound of it. Then there was another Akwanakai war cry and the muffled sound of a struggle. Soil tumbled around me, until I was convinced I would die, not with my skull crushed by an Iroquois war club, but smothered under tons of dirt.

The sounds ceased as abruptly as they had started. Minute after minute of silence passed. I began to struggle for each breath. The oxygen in the dank pit was fast being used up.

Eventually, the need for air outweighed my fear and I cautiously inched up the cover. Putting my lips to the crack, I breathed in gasp after gasp of air. Finally, hearing only the usual forest sounds, I found the courage to push the cover aside and climb out.

The breeze smelled heavily of smoke. As it changed direction the distant mourning cries of the women, an eerie wavering chorus of moans, reached me. Terrified I was going to find all those I loved among the dead, I joined the straggling parade of survivors that shuffled silent and stoop-shouldered toward the village.

I stifled a sob when I entered the clearing. There was nothing left of the wigwams but smoldering heaps. To the west, the cornfield was a carpet of smoking black ashes.

Women, men, and children stood in dazed clumps or milled frantically through the smoking debris searching for the remains of loved ones. I searched the grim faces, looking for my family.

"Becca, my child."

I spun toward Grandmother's voice and ran to her open arms. "Nemisa, Nowuk, Chumeka, their baby?" I asked, my voice trembling. "Are they still alive?"

"They live, though Nowuk is wounded."

Tears spilled onto my cheeks.

"No, child, there can be no time now for tears. Nowuk is strong as the bear. He will live to avenge his people. But, Granddaughter, there are many who need our help as much as Nowuk. Run, quickly now, to the hollow tree where I've cached my medicines. Hurry, Becca. There will be no rest until we have helped as many as we are able."

TEN

The following dawn, the people blackened their faces with ashes and, amid the slow throb of drums and wailing trill of the women, we carried our dead to the Sacred Hill. There we laid them beneath the earth, piling upon each new grave baskets of food, gifts of jewelry, a quiver of arrows, perhaps a toy or two for a child, all the items they would need for a journey along the Milky Way to the Land of the Dead.

Days passed. The arrow wound in Nowuk's shoulder healed. The women rebuilt their wigwams. The villagers who had left to meet the Hurons at the lake the Akwanakai called The Great Sea returned and mourning began anew as the newcomers heard the fate of their dead kin.

The moon had shrunk from the orange disk it had been the night of the Iroquois attack to a chalky crescent when the lookouts spotted Wanaga paddling his canoe up the stream. The canoe was mounded high, and the villagers noisily met him, crowding around the bank as he pulled it from the water.

From the back of the crowd, my hand tightly clutching Grandmother's, I stood on my tiptoes to peer above Nowuk's shoulder. Wanaga had on a cloth shirt, gaudy with bronze buttons and tattered, dirt-gray lace at the neck and sleeves. It was a strange contrast to the bear-claw necklace and scalp lock belt he still wore. With a look of hopeful expectation his glittering, black eyes swept slowly over the crowd. His face fell when he spotted me standing with Teepawn, and then grew fiercely hard. Grandmother met his glare and he looked away.

"My Akwanakai brothers, I have made contact with the Bear Faces, the strange, white-skinned tribe of the east." He waited until the gasps and exclamations subsided, then told them, "Although these people possess objects of great and wondrous medicine, they are not too proud to recognize that I, Wanaga, also have awesome exceptional medicine powers. In a great feast given in my honor, the Bear Face chief presented to me these gifts." Wanaga indicated the heavily laden canoe with a flamboyant gesture.

As the crowd elbowed and jostled each other for a better view, Wanaga called each of the council members forward one by one, conspicuously excluding Nowuk, and distributed to the men and their families all the marvels in his canoe—bronze kettles, calico cloth, bags of vividly colored glass beads, metal knives and axes—with the exception of a barrel keg of "spirit water." This he said was a ceremonial drink reserved for him alone, Bear Face medicine that enabled him to better communicate with his animal-spirit mentors.

The two greatest treasures he saved for last. He produced two shotguns—what the Akwanakai referred to as fire sticks—from the bottom of the canoe and, with a threatening flourish, held them high, seeming to relish the crowd's terrified gasp. No Akwanakai had ever possessed such powerful medicine, an object that could command thunder and lightning and would strike a man dead. The few fire sticks the people had seen had been in the hands of their enemies, the Iroquois. With pretentious formality he presented one fire stick to Okemaw who stood holding the musket as though Wanaga had just handed him a rattlesnake. The other fire stick Wanaga said he intended to keep for himself.

Old Muqua called out, "Wanaga, can you make the lightning strike that tree over there?"

"Alas, my brother, the black-powder medicine that summons the fire stick's thunder and lightning was stolen by Opacho, the evil manitou of the river. Jealous of my power, he attacked my canoe when I passed through the Great Rapids."

I tugged on Grandmother's sleeve and whispered in her ear, "The old liar! What happened is when that when he went over the rapids water splashed on his fire stick powder. It won't work if it's wet. Why don't you tell the people that?"

Grandmother held her finger to her lips. "I will say nothing, Granddaughter, and neither will you. It is best to let Wanaga trap himself in his own web of lies."

His face dour, Wanaga again scanned the circle of faces and said, "While I traveled in the land of the Bear Faces I had a terrible premonition of tragedy befalling my people. And now, as I look among you, my heart grows cold with dread, for so many faces I do not see."

I tugged again on Grandmother's sleeve and whispered, "I bet he's real broken up. Most likely disappointed that we weren't among the faces he didn't see."

"Shush, child, lest someone hear you. Never forget, Wanaga is still a man of great power and dangerous as a wounded grizzly. For that's exactly what we did, Becca, wound him."

Okemaw related to Wanaga the details of the Iroquois attack.

Wanaga gave out with a trilling moan. "Aiee! It is as I feared." With a sweeping gesture of his arm, he indicated the council members. "I warned, no, I pleaded with you on a day long ago, my council brothers, to heed my words, but did you listen to the voice of your protector and—"

"Wanaga, tread lightly. Remember I, too, issued a warning that day," Teepawn called out. Wanaga fixed his fierce glare on me. "Ah, but Teepawn, I had no intention of implicating your Iroquois granddaughter in the attack." His expression softened, his voice becoming the kindly benefactor as he played to the crowd. "I'll admit, Teepawn, in the past, we have had our grievances. But I, for the sake of village harmony, have always sought to put them aside. What a pity you can't find it in your heart to do the same. But, come now, let us speak of happier things. My Akwanakai brothers, you have mourned enough this past moon. Now I have returned, bearing wondrous gifts. Today, let us rejoice! Let us feast!"

A mighty cheer went up.

* * *

As had been the Akwanakai custom for generations, during the Month of Painted Leaves the village disbanded into smaller clan groups for the winter. Our family, along with six other households of the Beaver clan, packed our birch bark canoes with household goods and what food we had been able to harvest. Since the Iroquois had burned most of the fields, the harvest had been a meager one.

Our string of canoes paddled down the river for two days, bound for an area Nowuk had scouted out earlier and pronounced plentiful with game and far from enemy encampments. He said he had even spotted a few bison that were heading south, stragglers from the great herds roaming the southern prairielands.

In a clearing surrounded by massive maples and elms, the women erected a circle of wigwams. Nemisa and I gathered reeds from the riverbank and helped Grandmother weave extra wall mats. The wigwam walls had to have a double layer of thickness to insulate against storms. When the large wigwam we shared with Nowuk's family was snug and warm, the food caches had to be dug and filled with what little provisions we had salvaged after the attack.

Each day, when the sun set, all the families gathered outside around a fire, secure within the circle of wigwams, to sing and listen to the warriors and the old ones tell their stories. When I heard Grandmother begin a tale of an adopted granddaughter who risked her life by making herself a decoy and luring an enemy warrior away from her grandmother's trail, I felt my cheeks color, but savored the glow of pride. Grandmother mentioned no names. To do so would have been inappropriate and immodest, but from the approving glances I received, I realized no one doubted who the tale's heroine had been.

Suspended over the burning logs, a haunch of deer sizzled as Nowuk began a new tale. Little drops of fat dribbled down the crisping skin into the flames, sparking the air with a tantalizing aroma. I snuggled further down into the rabbit skin robe I shared with Nemisa and told myself I was happy here. Staring up at the black velvet sky and its glitter of stars, I could forget the lonely girl locked inside me who called softly, "I'm still me. I'm Becca...Becca Morrison." I swallowed the knot in my throat. Well, I could almost forget.

Days passed. The crisp autumn breeze became an icy whip lashing the tree branches, until they shed their last leaves of gold and scarlet. One morning, I awoke and found snow had dusted the wigwams and ice had crusted the water in the birch bark bucket. The sun, hiding behind a dismal blanket of gray clouds, was only a faint glow.

Was it November? Weather sure seems like it. That means Thanksgiving back home. I wonder if Mama and Daddy will miss me especially on that day? I pictured Mama putting the platter of turkey on the table and sinking into her chair to cry because their daughter was gone. Then it struck me. *What if, when Wanaga kidnapped me back to this time, I simply ceased to exist in the twentieth century?*

In fact, now, maybe Becca Morrison was never even born in Chicago . Mama and Daddy, Gramma and Grampa, they wouldn't be able to remember me, much less miss me, because I never existed in their time.

I stuffed my fist in my mouth so no one would hear me cry and ran toward the forest path. Sometimes I found that, if I ran hard enough and long enough, I could leave the scary thoughts behind me, at least for a while.

As the days grew shorter our band made preparations to move further south along the shores of the giant lake the Akwanakai called Michacoupee. The annual late fall trek was to seek out the small herds of bison that still roamed the plains south of the lake. The herds were becoming scarce there, but maybe this winter the Great Manitou would bless our hunt with a bison. The possibility was worth the perils and hardships the journey entailed. Also, the annual migration allowed the bands to meet, exchange news, trade and socialize before separating into small extended families and making their treks to winter campsites even further south.

After days of traveling overland, keeping the big lake's shore in sight, I could actually see the shoreline curving. Our group had reached the southernmost point of the western shore of Michacoupee, called Checagou, "place of the wild onion." Here the land was soft and dotted with bogs. Grandmother, Nemisa, and I, along with the other women and the children, tromped through the marsh with digging sticks and woven baskets strapped to our backs to harvest the wild onions which would be dried and used to season winter stews.

As I slogged through the marsh, wrinkling my nose at the foul smell, I paused to shift the weight of my burden basket, then scanned the horizon. Before me stretched the marshy wilderness dotted with the stooping figures of women and children, and behind me the blue expanse of Michacoupee with its froth of rippling white caps.

"Checagou" I softly mouthed. Could this possibly be Chicago? I remembered learning in school that Chicago was an Indian name. Three hundred or so years from now would there be skyscrapers, busy streets, thousands of people on this spot? I remembered taking the "L" train with Mama and Daddy to go see the Marshall Field's Christmas windows, and trembling as the train rumbled high above the streets and creaked around the sharp corners. And there were those hot summer days spent splashing in Lake Michigan's waves at North Avenue Beach. I brushed tears from my cheeks with a muddy hand and, sighing, bent to scoop up another onion with my digging stick.

Our group moved inland ten, maybe twenty, miles and soon reached our campsite, not far from a stream and settled in for the long winter. At night the wind was a raging, howling animal that battered and shook the wigwam, until I was certain the it was going to claw its way through the walls and devour us as we lay in our robes.

One morning, the buffalo robe that hung over the doorway would not yield outward. Nowuk had to tunnel his way out of a snowdrift that had buried the wigwam. Every day, wrapped in a buffalo robe, snowshoes on his feet, he set out with his bow to hunt. After a week without success, he finally returned with a deer slung over his shoulders, and that night we feasted, but not until Grandmother had first chanted a prayer of thanksgiving to the spirit of the deer for having given us his life.

No part of the deer was wasted. His hide made warm winter moccasins for our whole family, and new leggings and a shirt for Nowuk. The brains were boiled, mashed, and used to render the deer's hide to buckskin that was soft as any velvet. His intestines fed the dogs, and some of his bones made soup ladles, sewing needles, hair ornaments, and fishhooks. Grandmother put the last of the bones, picked clean, along with dried squash and roots, into a pot to make a thin soup. The sinew, stripped from his bone and muscle, became sewing thread, strung Nowuk's bows, and was used to repair the snowshoes we all had to wear in order to walk in the deep snow. Grandmother even blew the bladder up and tied the opening with sinew, to make a ball for baby Oocha to bat about as he crawled around on the wigwam floor.

Even though the air was so cold the trees snapped and cracked loud as a pistol shot, I found the early winter a happy time. My buffalo robe, worn hair side in and belted around my waist, kept me warmer than any twentieth-century coat ever had.

The deep snow became a wondrous playground. Quawno taught me to play a game called "snow snakes." We dragged a log through the snow to make a long, deep trough, its sides and bottom packed down smooth and ice hard. The object of the game was to throw a long smooth stick down the trough and make it travel further than anyone else's. The game got its name from the flexible stick that undulated like a snake, as it sped through the trough.

It seemed easy when I watched Quawno heave the stick. The first time I tried throwing the "snake" it glided only a few feet before it lodged in the snow. The other children waiting for their turns snickered and my cheeks colored. I turned in humiliation to go. Quawno grabbed my arm and gave the loudest of my mockers an angry look, shutting them all up.

"Give her a chance," he said. "All of you have been playing snow snakes since you left the cradle board."

He picked up the wooden stick and placed my hands on it and showed me how to rear back and get the most power in the throw. We practiced again and again, apart from the rest, until he gave me a grin and pronounced me ready to wield the snake with pride.

Later, Quawno and I bound strips of basswood bark to the soles of our moccasins and skated for hours on the rock-hard stream, giggling and laughing, even after we tumbled into a snow bank.

One day Nowuk made several sleds out of buffalo ribs bound with deer sinew. He harnessed two of the dogs to one of them, so they could pull Nemisa up the hill. I trudged through the snow in my snowshoes, dragging my own sled by a cord. At the top of the hill we joined Quawno and the other children, even some adventurous adults, in a breathtaking rollercoaster plunge to the bottom. Giggling and covered with snow, we waited for the dogs to trot down to meet us, so we could harness them up and do it all again.

As winter dragged on, though, I no longer had the energy for games. The food stores we had brought from the village began to shrink, then finally were gone. Other families, including Quawno's, moved to find more game south of the river. Before they left, Quawno came to say goodbye. He offered me a small piece of maple sugar candy, no more than a thumb's length, that he'd been saving.

I shook my head. "You should share that with your family."

"It's too small to split into so many pieces. You know how many brothers and sisters I have. "No, I want to share it with you as a sign of our friendship."

He broke the candy in two pieces and handed one to me. I savored the taste on my tongue, letting it slowly melt. Quawno shyly took my hand.

"May the Great Manitou keep you until we meet in the spring. Oh, and your family, too, " he quickly added.

My cheeks reddening, I smiled and squeezed his hand, remembering to mumble, "Thank you… and your family also." I turned to leave, my eyes glistening with tears I didn't want him to see.

More and more now we had to depend on the meat Nowuk brought home from the hunt, if we were to eat at all. Often, after a full day trudging through the snowbound forest, he appeared at the wigwam door, frost caking his face, and held only a thin rabbit or squirrel. But more often than not he appeared empty-handed. No mention, however, was ever made of the fact that he had returned without meat. Grandmother would simply chip off a large chunk from the block of river ice kept just outside the wigwam door and dump it into the previous night's broth.

I had never known what it was like to be truly hungry until that winter. Oh, I thought I'd been hungry on days when Mama had her PTA meetings and dinner was an hour late. Or the time I went on a Girl Scout campout and a raccoon broke into the cooler and ate all the frozen hamburgers.

No, I decided, that wasn't being hungry at all, but this was. I looked sadly at the faces of my Akwanakai family, as we sat around the flickering fire and sipped our cups of watery broth. Chumeka, her pretty face now sharp and gaunt, tried to get Oocha to nurse, but he only uttered a weak cry of frustration. She rocked him, her tears falling upon his tiny face and his black eyes big with hunger.

Grandmother boiled the last of the manoomin we had harvested moons ago from the small, reedy lakes in the north. She pounded a few strips of dried venison put aside for the sick, and mixed it all with her own cup of broth. Taking Oocha in her arms, she dipped her finger in the gruel and let him suck it from her finger. Though they all offered to give up a part of their own rations to help feed Oocha, Grandmother insisted she must be the one. Fighting tears, I announced that I, too, would not eat.

Grandmother, still strong enough to be feisty, sharply said, "Hush, child! I have seen many winters. If this one is to be my last, would you deny me the joy of giving this gift of life to my grandson?"

Chumeka wrapped her arms about me and let me sob against her shoulder until no more tears would come.

Day after day passed. Grandmother, her face now a skull molded over with crinkled copper, finally grew so weak she could only lie upon her robe. Nemisa and I took turns sitting at her side to give her an occasional sip of melted ice. When Grandmother called Chumeka to her and began to list what household items she would need for her journey along the Milky Way, I retreated to my sleeping platform and curled into a tight ball.

* * *

"Ayah!" Nowuk called out. "The Great Manitou has smiled upon us."

I looked up. Nowuk was standing in the wigwam doorway. Over his shoulder was slung a deer, little more than skin and bone, but meat all the same. Chumeka did the butchering, and Nowuk distributed portions of it to the other families, whose hunters had not been as fortunate. What was left became our feast of thick meat broth. Within days Grandmother was back on her feet and once again fully in charge of the household.

The days were lengthening now and the sun grew warm enough to melt the river ice. The men and boys sharpened their spears, and soon giant trout were sizzling over every hearth fire.

The winter had at last ended. But many seasons later, when the old ones told their tales around the fire, they spoke of that winter as the Time of the Ghost Moons, when many Akwanakai had died.

ELEVEN

Two winters passed. I grew tall, lithe, and strong. My body began to take on the soft contours of a woman. Grandmother announced the time had arrived for me to make a vision quest so I might become a full-fledged woman of the Akwanakai.

Though I solemnly nodded, I wanted to shout, "I don't want to be a woman, not yet. Just let me be a kid a while longer." No more games of stickball and snow snake, or joining Quawno and the other boys in their mock warrior games as they ran free through the forest. I wasn't ready to give up all of that. Grandmother, however, had decided differently.

So, one day at dawn, in a small, isolated wigwam within the forest, I sat naked upon a mat, with the panther necklace around my neck. Grandmother poured water onto the hot hearthstones and steam rose in great hissing clouds.

"Breathe deeply, child. You must purify your body and spirit. Make yourself worthy to receive a vision. The Great Manitou will disclose his mysteries only to those who seek him in fasting and solitude."

I swallowed and wondered what I would do if—in spite of my ceremonial sweat bath, fasting, and solitude—

the Great Manitou still found me unworthy and decided to deny me a vision.

Grandmother continued, "At dusk Nemisa will come to bring you a sacred bundle I have prepared for your vision quest. I go now to pray, seek out my own spirit mentor, the she-wolf. Return to my wigwam when three days have come and gone." She kissed my cheek and left.

Breathing deeply the hot steamy air, I closed my eyes and chanted over and over the prayer Grandmother had taught me.

Oh, Great Manitou, Mystery of Mysteries,
I hear your voice in the thunder,
The river's rushing waters.
The great oaks that whisper your name to the wind.

My spirit cries out,
And the heat of these stones,
Your sacred healing breath,
Refreshes and purifies me.

Behold I am now woman.
Bless me,
That my eyes may be opened this day,
That my spirit may know a sacred vision.

Minutes became hours. The sun's rays no longer filtered through the smoke hole and dusk was near.

Nemisa called out at the doorway, "My sister, I have come."

I awoke with a start. *Not even a full day, and already I'm dozing. The Great Manitou will never find me worthy.*

"May I enter?" Nemisa called timidly.

Holding my back rigidly straight, each hand resting palm-open upon a thigh as Grandmother had instructed, I answered with formality, "My sister, you may enter."

Nemisa laid two more branches upon the fire before she sat cross-legged beside me. She laid a bundle wrapped in buckskin on my lap. As was proper at such a sacred time, neither of us spoke. The only sound was the spit and crackle of the fire.

Nemisa made a move to rise, "My sister, I leave you with my blessings."

Breaking sacred decorum, I grabbed her wrist. "Oh, Nemisa, please don't go... not yet. I have to talk to you, please, just for a while." I chewed my lip, immediately embarrassed that I had burst out in such an unseemly manner.

Nemisa, confusion on her face, sank back down. "Well, I suppose, but I shouldn't stay long."

I swallowed hard, not sure how to broach such a sensitive and personal subject. "Nemisa, when you made your vision quest, did... well...did you fall asleep?"

"Oh, Becca, is that what you're worried about? Sure I did. Why, I bet even Grandmother fell asleep, at least once, when she made her vision quest."

I let out a sigh of relief. "I was so afraid I'd spoiled everything right from the beginning."

Nemisa gave my knee a reassuring squeeze. "You'll do fine."

I brushed my hand over the leather-bound bundle Nemisa had brought me. "Did Grandmother show you what was in this?"

Nemisa nodded. "I'm the one who brought the things from the cache where Grandmother had stored them all these many winters."

When I began to unwrap the first layer of leather, Nemisa said, "Maybe I should leave now?"

"No, Nemisa, stay just a little longer, please. After all, you are my spirit sister. I always share everything with you. What harm could there be?"

Uneasily, she consented.

I removed the last layer of leather covering from the bundle. There were my folded blue jeans and, beneath them, my dirty t-shirt. I felt a knot rise in my throat. "But I thought my Bear Face clothes had been burned with the wigwam when the Iroquois attacked that first summer."

"Grandmother never kept the shirt and leggings in our wigwam. She was afraid someone might find them and make trouble for you."

I felt in the pocket of my jeans and pulled out my broken glasses frame, one lens still intact. For a long instant, I stared at the glasses, wanting to believe there was something magical about this twentieth-century object of plastic and glass. I wanted to believe I could put them on and the girl I had once been would somehow materialize within a Michigan pine clearing, back in my own time . But, if that happened, would there be an Akwanakai woman-girl sitting now within this sacred wigwam awaiting her spirit vision? I needed to give life to both my selves, but how could that be without one ceasing to exist?

"My sister?"

I looked up with a start, having forgotten Nemisa sat at my side.

"What is that strange object you hold?" Nemisa asked.

"Of course, you never saw me in them. I used to wear them over my eyes, so I could see better. My eyes, like your twisted foot and arm, didn't work like they should when I was a Bear Face child." I put the glasses on my face. "See, I'll show you what I once looked like."

Nemisa pulled away with a gasp.

I giggled. "Oh, come on. I know I looked bad in glasses but surely not that awful."

"You look upon me with the evil eye!" Nemisa's hands flew to her face, covering her eyes. "Please, please, stop!"

I pulled the glasses from my face, and Nemisa regained her composure.

"My sister, why do you fear me?"

Nemisa's voice trembled. "Your eye grew huge and round like the one-eyed evil manitou, Aychuctu. He has only to look upon a person, and their body will shrivel and die."

"But, Nemisa, my eye only looks big because of the way the lens is shaped. Why don't you put on the glasses, and then you'll see how...how things change, look bigger."

Nemisa's face distorted with fear. "That thing has the power to change things to another form?"

"No, nothing like that. The glasses aren't magic or evil. They're just...." I floundered for the Akwanakai words that would explain without frightening her. "Oh, well, why don't you just try them on? Then you'll see what I mean."

Nemisa drew back in horror when I held the glasses out to her.

I stuffed the glasses back in the pocket of my jeans. "See, I've put them away." Tears misting my eyes, I glanced at Nemisa and asked, "Surely, you couldn't believe I would ever do anything to hurt you?"

The color gradually returned to Nemisa's cheeks. "No, I don't fear you, Becca. It's just that awful thing you put over your eye. It's...it's—"

"I won't wear them again. OK?"

Nemisa gave a relieved nod and, clearly anxious to change the subject, said, "Look beneath the Bear Face clothes, my sister, for Grandmother has bestowed upon you a truly wonderful gift."

I set aside the jeans and t-shirt, and an otter's face looked up at me. My eyes went wide. "But, that's Grandmother's sacred medicine bag."

The bag was fashioned from the hide of an otter, the head, tail, and paws still intact. Small painted black shells formed the eyes and nose. The whiskers were cords braided of brightly dyed milkweed fibers. Rainbow-painted shells dangled from the tail. The bag's opening was a slit down the otter's belly and was closed, shoelace style, with a rawhide cord. I knew the bag was one of Grandmother's most prized possessions, brought out from its hidden cache only on ceremonial occasions.

I searched Nemisa's face, wondering if she were hurt that Grandmother had chosen me to receive such a precious gift, but there was no jealousy in Nemisa's eyes.

Nemisa found my hand and gave it a squeeze. "Perhaps it is best, my sister, that I return now to the village."

After Nemisa let the robe fall back over the doorway, I placed the otter medicine bag across my thighs and reverently brushed my fingers over the peculiar lumps within. Did I have the right, I wondered, to peer inside? No, I decided, that right must remain Grandmother's alone.

I didn't know how long I stared unseeing at the dying fire but by the time I became aware of my surroundings again the sun had set. Only stars were visible through the smoke hole. The fire's last embers died and I sat in total darkness. To hear the sound of a human voice, I began to chant the prayer Grandmother had taught me. Hearing the hoot of an owl, I broke off in the middle of a word. Bad omen? Iroquois scout? Or perhaps simply a bird, an old hoot owl just as lonely as I was?

Without a fire, the wigwam was growing cold, but even if I had possessed the means, it was forbidden to ignite another fire in the hearth. Throughout the night I dozed fitfully, no longer feeling guilty but rather welcoming the respite sleep gave me from the cold.

As the hazy fingers of dawn touched the hearth stones, I awakened. I had been dreaming, but it was hardly the vision I had sought. I had been walking through the forest and came upon a stream. Kneeling, I scooped the sparkling, cold water into my cupped hands but, when I touched it to my lips, the water became hot sand.

Though I was now awake, the sensation I'd felt in the dream persisted. I licked my lips. They were dry and cracked, and this was only the beginning of the second day. Thoughts of food tormented me at first, but soon faded into insignificance when my thirst became unbearable. My tongue grew thick, rough as sandpaper. I could think of nothing but water—the way points of sunlight danced on river waves, the way water tasted on my tongue—cold, wet, delicious. Sleep became a wave that washed over me, only to cast me again upon a dry shore of wakefulness. Water swirled over the objects around me until their form was lost and they became only a meaningless blur of color.

This must be what dying is. Death was washing over me, pulling me deep beneath the waves and filling my veins with its cold, dark, seeping water. My mind slowed, numbed, but then strangely seemed to expand. I felt myself suspended in darkness.

Water, no longer cold, but warm and pulsing, was all around me. Contentment...peace...then a sudden rush of water, a pulsing, constricting pressure that would not relent. With the force of a slap, cold air hit me. Bright lights hammered their prickly points into my closed eyelids. I had been born.

* * *

When I woke the next day, I wrapped myself in a robe and, carrying the leather-bound bundle, staggered weakly into the village, making my way toward Grandmother's wigwam. The villagers I encountered turned their heads away, for it was bad luck to acknowledge one just returned from a vision quest until she had received her new name. When I entered the wigwam, all but Grandmother arose immediately and left.

Grandmother gestured for me to sit beside her at the hearth and handed me a cup of water. "Drink, child, that you may better speak."

I gulped the cool water.

Grandmother put a restraining hand on my arm. "Slowly, slowly, or your belly will knot with pain."

I forced myself to sip.

After a long silence, Grandmother asked me, "Did the Great Manitou bestow upon you the gift of a vision?"

It was an effort for me to make my swollen tongue form words. I spoke haltingly. "He did, Grandmother, but it was so strange, I don't understand."

"Tell me, child."

"At first I felt like I was dying, but it wasn't death." I stared into the fire, searching for the right words. "I think I was inside my mother's womb, then born. Yes, I'm sure that's what happened. But, somehow, I wasn't me. I don't even think I was human. I felt very small. I remember all was darkness. I must have been blind. An animal, big, warm, soft with fur, licked me with her gritty tongue and nestled me to her belly. One day my eyes opened and I found myself in a warm dark hole."

I paused, staring into the fire. "The vision is coming back to me more clearly, now. I can see a creature, my mother, I think, a beautiful golden panther with eyes that glowed yellow in the dark. I played with her tail and slept curled in a ball against her cushioned, white belly, her soft purr a pleasant buzzing in my ears. She brought me a half-dead rabbit."

My face clouding, I searched out Grandmother's eyes. "I didn't think it then, but now it seems so awful, Grandmother. I played with the poor wounded thing, batting at it with my paws until I finally sunk my teeth into its neck. Now, I shiver to think of what I did, how I felt. Grandmother, I actually savored the salty warmth of its blood on my tongue before I tore into the flesh of its belly."

"But that is not awful, child. You were a panther cub learning to hunt."

Giving a limp nod, I swallowed the knot in my throat and began again. "The day came when my mother took me outside the den. I remember the bright light blinded me at first, and I was frightened. But each time she took me out, I grew bolder. I chased butterflies, then birds and squirrels, wandering each day farther and farther from the den. I remember I had just trapped a mouse beneath a tree root when a crack of thunder shook the ground. I heard my mother scream. Then all was silent."

My voice faltered. Closing my eyes, I willed the tears not to fall. "Slowly, I slunk toward the den. Upon the wind, I tasted the scent, foul and sour, of some unfamiliar creature. When I peered between the branches of my hiding place, I saw a strange two-legged creature with white skin and a brush of yellow fur on its face and head. It squatted over my mother and cut off her tail. I waited until its foul scent had faded on the breeze. Then I slunk toward my mother. She lay very still. I butted her with my nose and paw, but she slept on. I curled within the crook of her belly, but her flesh soon grew cold.

I left when she no longer smelled of mother. After that day, I learned to hunt on my own. At first I went hungry, but as moons came and went, more often than not, I managed to fill my belly. I grew large and powerful. Seasons passed. I roamed the forest searching for a mate, but the two-legged creatures and their long, black death sticks had killed my panther tribe. At last it seemed I, alone among my kind, remained. I hated the two-legged ones. I stalked them and they stalked me.

"One day, I returned to the place of my birth. The flesh had left my mother's bones. Within the sheltering cage of her rib bones lay a small, wriggling, white creature with a fuzz of yellow hair upon its head. I sniffed the wind and smelled the foul scent of the two-legged ones. I crept toward my mother's bones, my teeth bared to sink deep into the neck of the two-legged cub."

The fierceness faded from my face, tears again welling in my eyes. "Grandmother, I wanted so much to hate that cub. I wanted to destroy it, as its tribe had destroyed mine. But I could not. My hate melted into love when I looked upon the cub. I took it and nurtured the cub as my own."

My voice trembled. "Grandmother, I was a panther, yet I took unto myself the very creature that destroyed my kind and sought also to destroy me." I choked on a sob. "I know, Grandmother, what the future will bring. The Bear Faces will destroy the Akwanakai, just as they destroyed the panthers. Am I wrong to want to love the very creature that I know will destroy my people?"

Grandmother gathered me into her arms and rocked me. "No, child, you are not wrong, for love is never wrong. You speak of guilt and betrayal. But I see another interpretation in your spirit vision. May I tell you?"

I gave a loud sniff and nodded.

"In your vision, you were born again as a panther. I see the spirit of Sawahna, your panther mother, stalking the forest. I see her die, and her cub—that is you—goes on to live. That cub survived, Becca, to became a she-panther, strong and powerful, and so will you. As the panther cub, you saw your tribe destroyed, experienced hate, craved revenge, yet in the end you chose love above all else. I see in that choice a healing of the selves, that war within you. Tribe against tribe. Perhaps those wounds shall also someday heal. Among the bones of your spirit mother, Sawahna, you found new life and chose to nurture it. You shall henceforth be called Che-no-a-wock-quai, or 'Woman Who Brings Forth Life.'"

Grandmother placed within my hands a small beaded-leather bag attached to a rawhide cord. Every Akwanakai adult, man or woman, who had made a vision quest wore such a medicine pouch tied around their neck. Tradition decreed that, after returning from the first vision quest, one must choose the amulets one's medicine pouch would contain. It was important to me that the pouch contain something of the sad, lonely White girl who still dwelled within me—Becca Morrison. The frame of my glasses was too big to fit, so I removed the one remaining lens and dropped it into the pouch. But now I needed something of Sawahna's.

Grandmother handed me the otter-shaped bag, the one Nemisa had brought to the ceremonial wigwam. "This sacred medicine bag belonged to Sawahna. Within it she kept her healing herbs and sacred amulets. With her last breath she begged me to keep it. All else went with her to the grave."

"But, Grandmother, Sawahna wanted you to have it, not me."

Grandmother's eyes took on a faraway look. "After all these winters, finally I understand. Sawahna did not give the sacred otter bag to me. No, she wanted me to save it for her. And now the time has come to return what she left in my trust." Grandmother placed my hand upon the otter skin. "Open it, Chenoawockquai, for it is yours…as always it has been."

My hand shaking, I unlaced the cords. Within were small leather pouches of dried herbs, a crude bone carving of a panther, painted shells, a bone whistle, feathers, and small smooth pebbles, each possessing the same peculiar living warmth of the panther pendant.

"Place each object within your palm," Grandmother said. "One, stronger than the rest, will call out to your spirit, and you will know that is the amulet to place within your pouch."

A small round pebble painted with a red circle drew me to it, and I dropped it into my pouch.

Grandmother nodded her approval. "Ah, the circle, a sacred symbol of harmony and peace. Now, something for the Akwanakai child you left behind you today in the ceremonial wigwam."

I pondered and then gave a shrug. "I don't know what to choose for her."

Grandmother arose, walked to the wall and withdrew a feather from a small niche hidden under the beam.

I raised my eyebrows in question. "A feather?"

"Ayah, but a special one, an eagle feather. The day of the Iroquois attack, when you saved my life, I found it on the trail. A warrior wears an eagle feather as a sign of proven courage. It is therefore a fitting amulet for the Akwanakai child you once were." Grandmother took her flint knife and cut off the tip of the feather, so it would fit into the pouch. The remainder of the feather she placed in the fire.

"Grandmother, what of Chenoawockquai? What shall I put in my medicine pouch for her?"

"She is a medicine woman, new-born. She must live a while first. In time, she will find her own amulet. We cannot force one upon her."

Solemnly, Grandmother tied the rawhide straps of the medicine pouch around my neck. "Chenoawockquai, may the Great Manitou guide your steps to walk forever in the paths of love and peace. And so may the Medicine Circle of death and life be complete."

.

TWELVE

My new name took some getting used to. Though I thought the symbolic meaning of Chenoawockquai beautiful, hearing the sounds strung together in one sing-song mouthful made me think Grandmother had intended to name, not a girl, but a new species of dinosaur. I was relieved when, for the sake of practicality, Grandmother shortened my ceremonial name to Chenoa. Now, after a winter's passing, I no longer mourned my childhood name. I knew that Chenoa, the Akwanakai child, was secure deep within me, just as Sawahna and the White girl, Becca, were.

I gave myself over to the gentle dip and pull rhythm of the canoe paddle. The cool, spring breeze gently tugged at my braids and rippled the fringe of my buckskin shirt. A few isolated mounds of snow still dotted the riverbank and sparkling beads of sunlight danced upon the waves. I took a deep breath inhaling the scent of wet earth, rich with the promise of new life.

As the canoe rounded a turn in the river, I saw a doe drinking at the water's edge, her fawn at her side. The doe looked up with a start and, for an instant, froze. The canoe was so close that I could see the doe's eyes, soft and brown, yet huge with terror. In a tawny blur of motion, the two vanished into the forest. I smiled, glad I had been the one to come upon the deer and not the men and boys whose canoes were just rounding the bend in the river. Although I loved roast venison, it would have saddened me to see the pretty doe fall, an arrow piercing her side.

Traditionally, as soon as the snow had thawed, and just before new leaves hazed the tree branches pale green, our women and children set off in a caravan of birch bark canoes for the maple sugar camp. A detachment of the younger warriors, our protectors against the Iroquois, always accompanied us.

When we reached the grove of sugar maples, we banked our canoes, with the air of jubilant guests arriving for a feast. The children, laughing and shouting, spilled onto the river bank, running this way and that, managing to blunder into everyone's path. But no one seemed to mind. The sugar camp was always a happy place. The starving moons of winter at last were over. Seeing the canoe carrying Grandmother and Nemisa nearing the bank, I waded into the frigid water to help them pull it ashore.

Grandmother waved me aside. "No, Granddaughter, we can manage the canoe, but go help Chumeka with that heavy kettle."

Chumeka, her belly beginning to noticeably round with her third child, was tugging a huge iron kettle up the slippery bank and not making much headway. Clinging to her skirt was her daughter of three winters, Nanee. Oocha, his toy bow and a quiver of arrows slung over his shoulder, was standing behind the kettle, his little round face scrunched tight with the effort of pushing.

I stood beside him. "Come on, Oocha. We'll push together."

After the canoes were unloaded and a crude brush lean-to was erected, I looked about for a place to rest. On a gentle slope overlooking the campsite, I spotted Nemisa alone beneath a maple and set out to join her. It was becoming more difficult for Nemisa to get around. Two winters ago, her spine had begun twisting into an "S" curve, and now being on her feet for long periods had become a painful ordeal. Although the hard physical labor of the sugar camp was impossible for her, she did her part by caring for the infants in cradleboards and telling stories to the younger children.

With a yawn, I sank down beside her and leaned back against the massive tree trunk. "Where did all the little ones go?" I asked.

As though in answer, a sudden chorus of high-pitched war whoops and children's squeals came from the forest.

Nemisa gave a laugh. "Sure sounds like they're off making war on the poor chipmunks and squirrels. And Taniya and Paneek just took their babies to nurse them, so for a while I'm free." She handed me a small basket of red berries, no bigger than beads. "Oocha found them for me, the first berries of the season. Go ahead, have some. They are sour, but at least they will quiet the rumble in your belly."

I popped a handful in my mouth and began to chew. I pinched my face into a scowl and forced myself to swallow. "Sour doesn't even come close. They're awful!"

"Oh, come on, they're not that bad. Hey, Chenoa, before the victorious chipmunk warriors return, I want to show you something." Nemisa cleared the dead leaves from a patch of earth. Taking a sharp stick, she began to scratch letters into the dirt. "The song of the ..." Her forehead furrowed with concentration as she struggled with the English word. "Chenoa, what is the Bear Face word that means 'injured'?"

"Why do you want to tell your story in the tongue of the Bear Faces? Just use Akwanakai words. Wouldn't that be easier?"

"Too easy. I must use the Bear Face words."

"Nemisa, that doesn't make any sense."

"Sure it does. When I have to dig and search in my mind for words, it makes me forget for a while the pain."

My voice grew soft with concern. "Your back is bad today?"

Nemisa put on a cheerful smile. "Ah, it's just from kneeling so long in the canoe. You know, my legs get all cramped. Tomorrow I'll be better. But you never answered me. What's the Bear Face word for 'wounded'?"

"Well, you could say 'hurt.'" I suggested.

"No, for a song, 'wounded' sounds better," she said, her brow furrowed in thought.

Nemisa scratched the letters, 'w-o-o-n-d-e-d' into the dirt.

I thought a moment, then smoothed out the second 'o' with my finger and substituted 'u.'

"Why did you do that?" Nemisa asked. "'Food,' 'moose,' 'root.' They all have the sound of 'oo.'"

"Trust me, it's 'ou' this time."

Nemisa shook her head with disgust. "And you tell me some times I make no sense!"

I laughed. "I know what you mean. I felt the same way when I was learning picture words."

Nemisa picked up the stick again but hesitated.

"Need help with the next word?" I asked.

"No, I know what picture marks to use, it's just...oh, it's foolish to write out my song." She made a move to smear out the words she had just written.

I grabbed her hand. "Why are you scratching it out? What's wrong?"

"You know how each warrior has a song that tells of his deeds in war or the hunt? Well, I wanted to make my own song, the story of me Nemisa. In my song, I am the mourning dove, my wing wounded. And one dawn, I sing a prayer, asking the Great Manitou to make me whole, so I, like the eagle, can soar up to the sun. And, well, it goes on, but... guess I want my own song, just to be able to say I walked upon this earth, that I breathed, I laughed, I cried, I lived once, too. Oh, I know I can never sing it before the fire as the warriors do their songs, but somehow... I thought... the picture marks... maybe that will be my way to sing my song. Foolish, huh?"

"No, it's not foolish at all," I said. "Go on, make the next word."

Nemisa let out a deep sigh. "Oh, I don't know. Guess I need to sing it in my head some more, before I make the picture words. Are you sure you don't think it's foolish?"

I gave her a hug. "I'm sure."

Nemisa smiled and stuffed a handful of berries in her mouth. She offered the basket to me. "Want some more?"

I gave my head a vigorous shake.

"Oh, but they taste good the way Grandmother cooks them. She slices cattail root and then mashes the berries and puts..." She glanced at me as I shaded my eyes, staring intently toward the river where a canoe was fast approaching. "Hey, Chenoa, did you hear anything of what I just said?"

"Huh?"

"Well, guess that answers my question."

When the canoe neared the riverbank, the young warrior paddling it jumped into the water and, with great effort, shoved his craft ashore. I realized why he'd struggled so hard with the canoe when he pulled a yearling buck from it and, with a loud grunt, slung it over his shoulders.

"Ayah!" I said, "See what a fine deer Quawno has killed!"

Nemisa giggled. "The way your eyes glow, could it be, not the four-legged buck you admire, but rather the two-legged one?"

My cheeks colored. "You know, Nemisa, I keep telling myself, 'Accept that Quawno isn't interested in you anymore.' When I look his way, he just turns his head away from me. When we pass on the path, he won't say anything to me. Every time I see him, what do I do? I think about how strong and tall he's become, how handsome his face is. I remember all the stick ball games, the sled races we used to have, how he practiced with me over and over, so I could throw the snow snake straight and true. Then all I want to do is cry. Remember, Nemisa, how he even braved the other boys' teasing and taught me how to hunt with his own bow and arrow, just because I begged him to?"

"But, Chenoa, boys grow to be men. For him, to do such things with you now would be unseemly. And, so it would be for you, too. What would all the gossips say if you were to go disappearing into the forest with Quawno from dawn to dusk, like you used to do when you were children? Do you believe they would accept that he was simply teaching you to hunt? Have no doubt those old crones would hoot and jeer the moment you stood in the maidens' circle at a feast."

"Well, Nemisa, no need to fear for my reputation. Quawno doesn't even glance my way anymore, much less run off with me to the forest."

"But there have been others who have courted you."

"Ayah, there was Pocheko who has a face like a weasel. And then there was the one who strutted about like a pheasant in mating season and had the brain of a bird."

"But, Chenoa, what of Keokuk? He's a great warrior and hunter. With him, you would never lack for meat, even during the coldest winter."

I wrinkled my nose. "But, Nemisa, he's an old man!"

"Oh, not that old…just has a little gray hair is all. And since he has two other wives, you would have someone to share the work with."

I teasingly raised one eyebrow. "Ayah, almost sounds like you want to marry me off and be rid of me."

"My sister, what an awful thing to say. I will miss you terribly when you leave Grandmother's wigwam to marry." Nemisa's eyes grew moist. "Now me? I know I will never marry. No man would want a wife that's a cripple. But you? Chenoa, you can have a life—children, a husband who will love and provide for you. You have only to find the man. Just get it out of your head that Quawno is the only one for you."

I watched Quawno saunter over to join the other warriors lounging on mats around the fire and gave a loud humpf. "You're right, I don't need Quawno. Fact is, I don't need a husband at all. Oh, I know it's not fair to expect Nowuk to continue providing for me. After all, soon he will have three children to feed. But I can hunt, probably as well as Quawno can. No reason why I can't provide meat for the three of us - you, Grandmother, and me."

"But, Chenoa, I'm sure Nowuk doesn't mind providing for you, besides you can't…Chenoa?"

I stared into space, my thoughts blocking out Nemisa words. Doing the hunting makes perfect sense. *Why didn't I think of it sooner? I won't be a burden on Nowuk anymore, and I won't have to marry someone I don't want to. Who knows? Maybe someday I'll even be able to walk past Quawno and not feel a knot rise in my throat.*

Nemisa tugged at my sleeve. "You're not listening again, are you?"

"To what?"

Nemisa gave a sigh of exasperation. "To what I've been saying. All right, I'll repeat it. Wanaga is just waiting for you to do something that he can twist and distort and use to condemn you. An Akwanakai woman who refuses to marry and decides, instead, to take on the tasks of a man would be looked upon with much suspicion."

"But why?"

"Who can say why? It's just not the Akwanakai way. When Wanaga sees that, he will speak ill of you, play upon the villagers' fears, and soon he will have some of them believing you are possessed by an evil manitou."

"He wouldn't dare make trouble. He knows Grandmother would accuse him of robbing Sawahna's grave. She has that to hold over him."

"But, Chenoa, he will say it is his word against yours, and what is the word of one possessed?"

I clenched my fists. "If anyone is possessed by evil, it's Wanaga." I was silent for many moments lost in thought. "Nemisa, don't you think it an odd coincidence that each time the Iroquois have attacked, Wanaga has been away on one of his mystery expeditions?"

"What are you saying? He betrays us to the Iroquois? But why should he? When the enemy burns our crops, Wanaga goes hungry also."

"Aw, think about it, Nemisa. Shortly after a raid, that's when he usually appears with a canoe full of Bear Face goods to give to those whose favor he seeks. Now why should the Bear Faces give Wanaga gifts?"

"He says the Bear Face chief respects his medicine powers and knowledge."

"Now that's a lie if I ever heard one! I remember from my life among the White men that they respected very little about the Indians and most certainly not what they would have considered a crazy old medicine man's conjuring. No, there's some other reason."

"But Chenoa, why should the Bear Faces reward him for betraying us? What is it to them whether the Akanakai live or die?"

"Remember what Grandmother told us, that many harvests ago, an Iroquois warrior took only the scalp of another warrior, never the scalp of a woman or child. Now, more often than not it is the women and children they scalp."

Nemisa spat with disgust. "And the Iroqois call themselves fierce warriors? What honor can there be in taking the scalp of a child?"

"That's what I mean. The Iroquois are taking scalps, not for honor, as our warriors do, but for some other reason. A true story is told in my White tribe's picture marks. It tells of a band of Bear Faces called the English who gave the Iroquois gifts in return for the scalps of their Indian enemies."

"But Chenoa, why would the Bear Faces want the scalps of the Akwanakai? We have done their tribe no harm."

"I don't think that matters to them. The Bear Face, especially now judge enemies by the color of their skins rather than by their deeds. You know, Nemisa, the more I think about it, I'm sure Wanaga's gifts whether from the English or the Iroquois are tributes for the scalps of his own people."

Nemisa shivered. "How can a man do such an evil as betray his tribe? And yet... " Her voice trailed off. "Perhaps, yes, perhaps there is truth to your suspicions. Though there is nothing we can say to prove his guilt. For how could you go before the council and tell them what you have just told me? Can you speak of Bear Face picture marks or your knowledge of what is yet to be?

I shook my head. "Please, Nemisa, let's not talk of Wanaga anymore. So much power and evil in one man frightens me."

* * *

I thought of our conversation later, as I stirred thick, golden maple syrup bubbling in a kettle. My arms ached, and I stopped to wipe the sweat from my forehead.

Grandmother, her knife in hand, sat on a mat nearby, hollowing out a bass wood trough. It would later be one of many already fastened to the trunks of maples to funnel the sweet, trickling drops of golden sap into a birch bark bucket.

Stepping back from the fire, I breathed the cold air like a tonic. Longingly, I looked toward the forest where the children were squealing with laughter, chasing each other among the trees.

Grandmother looked up and followed my glance. A gentle smile spread over the old woman's face. "Granddaughter, you have been stooped over the kettle since early morning. Too long for a young woman. You'll end up like me, a back curved as a turtle's shell. I'll stir for a while. Need to uncramp my legs anyway."

She handed me a small hatchet. "Search the woods, Granddaughter, and test the maples we haven't bled yet. Remember just a single, sharp hatchet blow to the trunk. If sap dribbles from the wound, the maple is ready to give us her lifeblood."

Fastening the hatchet to my belt, I responded with a grin, grateful for the freedom Grandmother was offering me. I longed to bolt toward the forest at a run, bounding over the dead branches like a deer, the way Becca would have. After glancing toward the circle of women, I decided a fast walk would have to do, at least until I was out of view of the campsite.

I slowed as I passed the men lounging on fur robes, playing a noisy game of dice. Their loud voices and laughter drowned out the women's chatter, even the squeals of the children squabbling over a ladleful of maple syrup. From the corner of my eye, I caught sight of Quawno. For an instant, I thought he had glanced my way as I walked by. My breath quickened, and I felt that familiar tightness in my chest that Quawno always triggered. I longed to look over my shoulder and see if he was staring after me, then chided myself for indulging in wishful thinking. Setting my lips in a tight line, I told myself I didn't care anymore about Quawno, anyway.

Once the forest closed in around me, I broke into a run down the path, reveling in the freedom, the breeze blowing through my hair, the soothing rhythm of movement, the exhilaration. When my breath began to come in hard gasps, I slowed to a comfortable lope, finally stopping when I came to a sunlit clearing.

I found a relatively dry spot beneath a tree and stretched out on my back, pillowing my head on my arms. The tree's branches were festooned with wild grape vines, the thick woody cords dangling almost to the ground. I wondered if the vines would be strong enough to hold my weight. It might be fun to try swinging on them.

An image came to my mind of a poplar tree with silvery leaves, a swing dangling from one of its lower branches. A girl, with glasses slid low on her nose and long, stringy, brown braids, sat on the swing's wood-plank seat. She kicked off her sandals. She wanted to feel the wind between her toes. Higher and higher she swung, until finally, she could touch the clouds. Tears in my eyes, I shook off the vision. I wanted—no, needed—to keep those memories alive, but the pain, would it ever completely fade without the memories fading, too?

I sat up, casting about for something that would lighten my mood. My eyes lit again on the grape vines. Why not try making a swing? I jumped to my feet and tugged tentatively on one. It seemed attached securely enough. Putting my entire weight on it, I swung back and forth a few times. It held. But I wanted something a little closer to the Bear Face swing I'd had as a child. I noticed one vine seemed longer than the rest, dangling from a high branch, then draping over and under the tree's lower branches.

I could see that, if I climbed the tree, I would be able to untangle that vine. Then it would be long enough to loop around and fasten to the branch across the way. I smiled. *Hey, I'd have myself a swing with a seat after all.*

Bunching up my skirt thigh-high, I secured its folds under my belt and perused the tree, looking for the best place to start my climb. I hoisted myself up to a crook in the two lower branches and, settling myself in, started to untangle the vine.

"Chenoa?" It was a man's deep voice.

I looked down into Quawno's upturned face and cringed.

"Chenoa, why are you sitting in that tree?"

I tried to think of an acceptable reason for a full-grown Akwanakai woman to be sitting on a tree branch. How about saying that I'd been treed by a bear? No, a hunter with any eyes at all would never fall for that. No bear tracks. How about claiming that I'd been searching for bird eggs? Every spring, the Akwanakai raided the riverbank nests of geese and ducks. Why not something a little smaller, a nest in a tree?

I tried to make my voice sound very mature and dignified. "The tree? ...I...uh, I was searching for a thrush's nest so I could get her eggs."

"But why?"

"Well, to cook and eat, of course!"

"Chenoa, do you know how small thrush eggs are?"

"So, does that matter?"

Quawno just smiled.

I swung down to the ground and confronted him, my hands on my hips.

"All right, I wasn't really looking for a thrush's nest. I just said that so you wouldn't think me foolish for sitting up in a tree." I realized that he was staring at my bare legs and quickly pulled my skirt down.

A smile again twitched on his lips. "So, why then were you up in the tree?"

I drew in a deep breath and decided to risk the truth. "I was trying to untangle the vines so I could make something to swing on."

He began to laugh.

My eyes flashed fire. "Well, what's so funny about that? Maybe I'd like to have some fun, too. If you can play dice, guess I can make a swing if I want to."

"Forgive my laughter, Chenoa. I guess it just pleasures me to know you have not changed all that much since we were children."

"Well, it's for sure you've changed!"

His face fell. "I no longer please you? There is another you would rather have court you?"

Forgetting decorum, I stared him full in the face. "You want to court me?"

Noticeably flustered, he looked away. "Well, yes. Why else would I follow you into the forest? It was my intention to ask if you would allow me to visit some time at the wigwam of your Grandmother."

"But, Quawno, since I made my vision quest you have barely spoken to me. I thought you were avoiding me."

He hesitated. "Actually, I was avoiding you. You became a woman, a beautiful one, at that, and you are granddaughter to a great medicine woman. Ay! Who was I? One not even a warrior yet. I vowed I would not approach you until I had proven myself on the warpath and avenged my father's death upon the Iroquois, and now that I have returned from my first war party, bloodied my—"

"Don't tell me about men you've killed. I don't want to hear about it."

His face grew solemn. "I know how you feel, Chenoa. It pained me also to think perhaps one of the men I must face and kill might be the father or brother of the woman I love."

I longed to explain to Quawno that I was not Iroquois, to tell him about my true origins, but the words would not come. Fear that the truth would drive him away stopped me. I settled for, "Don't worry, Quawno. There's no possible way you could ever kill any of my kin, for they are in a land beyond any Akwanakai arrow or war club. They have been born to the world beyond."

I said that, knowing my ambiguous words would mislead him into believing all my relatives dead. *But, in reality Mama, Daddy, Gramma and Grampa are all dead...to me, anyway. It's not a lie I'm telling you, Quawno.*

He made a move, as if he would put his arm around my shoulders to comfort me, but stopped abruptly. For a man not yet officially a suitor to touch a maiden in such a way would be an affront to not only the girl but to her family as well.

He swallowed hard. "Chenoa, may I meet with you again?"

I felt my eyes brim with tears of happiness. "I would be honored."

THIRTEEN

Using a flint knife, I painstakingly sliced a tiny moccasin sole from a length of velvety buckskin. I was making a pair of ceremonial moccasins for Chumeka's newborn son to wear for his Naming Feast. On that day Nowuk would hold the child up to the four winds, asking the Great Manitou to bestow his blessing upon his infant son. The moccasins I was making were to symbolize the path of honor and courage the child would follow as he walked the earth.

I held up the small oval of buckskin. "Well, Grandmother, what do you think? Is it too small?"

Grandmother looked up from the basket she was weaving. "Ah, no, it's a perfect size for such a tiny warrior."

I added another branch to the hearth fire. Although it was late spring, the night wind was blowing unseasonably cold and blustery against the wigwam walls. We heard a thud, the sound of something heavy being dropped just outside the wigwam.

A voice called through the fur robe that covered the doorway. "A man comes bringing a deer to the wigwam of Teepawn, grandmother to the woman Chenoawockquai."

My face lit up at the sound of Quawno's voice, even though he sounded rather formal. I made a move to rise.

Grandmother put a restraining hand on my arm. "Do not go to him," she whispered. "There is a proper way to do these things, you know. You must not appear too eager." Grandmother walked to the doorway and spoke with Quawno, keeping the fur robe between them. "An old woman thanks you for your kindness to herself and her two granddaughters."

I listened to Quawno's footsteps fade, and my face fell. "Shouldn't you have asked him to come in or something?"

"Of course not," Grandmother said, ambling back to sit before the fire. "Asking him in wouldn't be proper. This is a serious betrothal Quawno proposes. This is not just another one of his little wigwam visits." Grandmother leaned toward me, narrowing her eyes in mock indignation. "Nor one of those sneak meetings in the forest you two have been having lately."

I shot an accusing glance at Nemisa who was trying to smother a giggle behind her hand.

Nemisa vigorously shook her head. "I swear, Chenoa, I never told her anything."

"Nemisa didn't have to tell me anything. Did you think I was always a bent, wrinkled, old woman with a face like a snapping turtle?" She smiled into the fire, her black eyes dancing. "No, I, too, was a young woman once, and so much in love with my handsome warrior. Ayah, what memories!" Her expression grew serious as she crossed her arms over her chest. "But now, Chenoa, we must talk of you and Quawno."

"But, Grandmother, shouldn't we bring in the deer he brought us?"

"That is what we must talk about. If we take within our wigwam his gift of a deer, that means you are betrothed to him. No other man may court you. Until next spring, you will continue to live as a maiden in our wigwam. During that time Quawno must furnish us with fresh meat to prove himself able to provide for a family. And you, in turn, must sew his garments, make his moccasins, show yourself proficient in the skills of a wife. Ayah, be assured, Granddaughter, that Quawno's mother will be judging you."

I sobered as I thought of my mother-in-law to be, a large, lumpy-hipped woman with a face sour as the first berries of spring.

Grandmother studied me. "Oh, don't worry, child. Quawno's mother may seem a bit gruff at times, but she has a generous spirit."

I nodded uneasily.

"Well, Granddaughter, if you are unsure, then Nowuk can politely return the deer to Quawno's mother with our regrets, and Quawno will understand you have refused his betrothal offer. You will be free to court another."

"NO! I will be Quawno's wife!"

Grandmother's face beamed. "Well, then it would seem we have a deer to butcher. And much to do before the spring!"

* * *

The early autumn sun was still hot as it beat down on my head. The sand burned my feet through the rawhide soles of my moccasins, but those things went unnoticed. Tears in my eyes, I looked out over the lake the Akwanakai called Michacoupee, the Great Sea, and knew I was standing on the shore of Lake Michigan, probably on what would one day become the Chicago beaches. There was no mistaking this lake. The blue, heaving water stretched to the horizon and the frothy whitecaps slapped the rushes growing along the muddy shoreline. So many times Mama and Daddy had taken me to the beaches at North Avenue or Montrose. Would this wilderness of swampland become one of those beaches? We were on the southern end of the western shore of Michacoupee, so perhaps it was true?

Closing my eyes, I had the eerie sensation that, when I opened them, the sand would extend farther inland and be covered with a multi-colored patchwork of beach blankets. Sunburned kids would be building sand castles. I would smell the suntan lotion, the vendor's hot dogs, and hear the excited babble of English, the squeals of children splashing in the icy waves, and a transistor radio blaring rock and roll.

Quawno's voice broke through my reverie. "Michacoupee, it is a beautiful lake, isn't it?"

Opening my eyes, I reached for Quawno's hand. "Very beautiful."

He stroked my cheek, his fingers coming away wet with my tears. "You've been crying. Why are you sad?"

"Oh, I just get that way sometimes. Kind of hard to explain why."

He put his arm around my shoulders, and I rested my head against his chest. "I fear," he said, "my mother will click her tongue at us if she sees us." A teasing smile twitched his lips.

"Your mother does take her chaperoning job seriously, doesn't she?"

Quawno laughed. "Well, she promised Teepawn she would."

I glanced toward a gentle slope where our band was setting up their lean-to wigwams. In the distance, I could hear the women's happy chatter intermingled with Okemaw's deep voice bellowing orders, dogs barking, babies crying, and the shouts and laughter of children.

I had accompanied Quawno and his family, along with a sizable portion of the rest of their band, to the annual autumn trade gathering. The event was a joyous reunion that included many bands from a radius of hundreds of miles. Akwanakai, Huron and Neshnabe–the tribe the whites would later call Potawatomi–would meet with kinsmen from other groups to exchange news, trade goods, renew love affairs, and attend feast after feast. This was the place where the warriors, painted and bedecked in their finery, staged stick ball games that pitted one band against another in violent competition. Some men were known to gamble away an entire year's accumulation of furs on the outcome of a single wrestling match, foot race, or stick ball game. Though I had never attended the gathering before, from what Grandmother had told me, I imagined it possessed all the color and excitement of the Michigan State Fair that Grampa had taken me to every summer.

Yet I had mixed feelings about going. I worried about Nemisa and Grandmother left behind with the other villagers. Early autumn, just before the harvest, was often the time of Iroquois attacks. When Nemisa hadn't been well enough to make the long canoe ride to the trade gathering, Grandmother insisted she had also become too feeble to make the trip, though I suspected that Grandmother would have relished going along if it weren't for her concern for Nemisa.

When I had suggested that perhaps I, too, should remain in the village, Grandmother spoke up, her voice emphatic, "No, it is your place to go with your husband-to-be and his family. Now, don't worry about us. With Nowuk remaining here and half the other warriors, too, we'll be just fine. Now, go on with you, and have fun." She narrowed her eyes and glared mischievously. "But, not too much fun. I will not have my granddaughter hooted out of the maiden's circle at the Harvest Feast."

The memory brought a smile to my face.

Quawno gave my hand a squeeze. "Ah, at last, you smile."

A young boy's voice called out, "Quawno, Quawno, come quick!"

We looked toward the voice. It was Quawno's younger brother, Pawho. He was running full speed toward us, waving his arms and screaming as if a war party of Iroquois were on his trail. "Quawno! You're going to miss them!" The boy, his chest heaving, skidded to a stop in front of his brother.

"Miss what?"

"The Bear Faces! Wanaga brought them, here. And, Quawno, they are every bit as ugly as the Hurons say. Long fur on their chins and under their noses. One even has big round eyes the color of lake water. And the smell?" He wrinkled his nose. "Whew! Sour as beaver musk!"

I stood scarcely breathing. Wanaga. I had so hoped he was gone for good. He still had the power to terrify me. I knew he meant to harm me, my family, and my people. Was he now allied with the White men? Those people with hair on their faces and pale eyes seemed alien to me to me now. Yet the Becca of the twentieth century would have seen them as her people. I looked toward Quawno, the sculpted arch of his nose, the high cheek bones, the polished bronze of his skin, his eyes, warm and brown, his long hair, black and glossy as a crow's wing. No, this man was of my race, my people.

I searched out his hand and gripped it tightly. Lowering his voice, Pawho whispered, "I think Bear Faces must not be as smart as human men. Do you know what Okemaw said? The Bear Faces call us "pot-a-wa-ta-mee."

Quawno appeared puzzled. "But why? That means in Huron, 'the people prepare a fire.'"

Pawho giggled. "See what I mean. The Bear Faces are stupid. Okemaw said one Bear Face pointed to our campsite and asked the Huron, the one who makes talk for them, 'What tribe of men is that?' The Huron said, 'You mean, over there? The people who prepare a fire?'" Pawho paused for emphasis, so the punch line wouldn't be lost on his brother. "I guess the Huron must have told them after that, 'Ah, yes, those people who prepare a fire, they are of the Akwanakai tribe.' But, Quawno, the Bear Face was so stupid, he heard only 'Potawatomi' and now, Okemaw says the Bear Faces think that is our name. Come quickly Quawno or you will miss all that happens." The boy turned and ran back toward the rapidly expanding crowd.

Quawno gave a hearty laugh. "So, now we are all Potawatomi, huh? Well, I suppose it hardly matters what the Bear Faces choose to call us."

I smothered a laugh into my hand, wishing I could share Pawho's joke with good old Charlene Boersma. I told myself it was foolish that Charlene's words still bothered me after all these years, but they did. I could still hear Charlene's taunting sing-song, "Hey, Becca, just what tribe is this Indian of yours supposed to be from, anyway?"

And I heard my voice say, "Akwanakai."

Charlene's gleeful snort that day still rankled me. "Humpf! That just shows how much you know, Becca Morrison! The Potawatomi and Hurons were the only tribes that lived in this part of Michigan."

At last, Becca has been vindicated. It's too bad though that Charlene Boersma will never know. Becca would have had such fun making her eat her words. I glanced at Quawno, and the smile faded from my face. *No, the Bear Faces are far from the half-witted curiosities Pawho considers them. They could be deadly.*

"Please, Quawno, don't go near the Bear Faces. Stay here with me, instead."

He gave me a patronizing smile. "But, Chenoa, what is there to fear? I promise, if you go with me, I won't leave your side. Surely, you wouldn't want to miss such a strange sight? You may never get another chance to be near the Bear Faces.

Oh, Quawno, if you could only know. Reluctantly, I agreed to go see the Bear Faces. It was clear that Quawno was determined, and I didn't want to be left alone with my thoughts. I needed to quiet those voices that were clamoring to whisper their memories and tug at my spirit.

Quawno's physical presence, his hand in mine, always silenced the voices, grounded me here in this time.

Minutes later, still clinging to Quawno's hand, I stood at the fringe of the boisterous crowd. My future mother-in-law, breathless, came ambling up to stand beside us.

She tugged on my sleeve. "You're taller than me. Can you see them?"

I stood on my tiptoes but could still see nothing more than a sea of heads, feathers, and bronze backs.

Quawno's brother wormed his way through the crowd, shouting all the while, "My brother! Quawno! I must talk to you. QUANO!"

Quawno glared at the boy. "Hush, Pawho, you embarrass your family with such unseemly squealing."

Undaunted by the scolding, the boy said, "But, Quawno, I have a message from Okemaw." He stopped to get his breath, then continued, deepening his voice importantly. "Wanaga has called upon Okemaw as chief of our band to meet with the Bear Faces. Okemaw has summoned two of our warriors to accompany him." The boy broke into an exuberant, wide-mouthed grin. "One of them is you, Quawno! And he said the warrior's families may go, as well." He gave an involuntary leap of joy. "We're going to see the Bear Faces. And up close, too!"

Moments later, I looked at Quawno, head held high, as he stood beside Okemaw and another young warrior. If it was Okemaw's intention to impress the Bear Faces, I thought he had chosen well in Quawno. He, like the other warrior chosen to represent us, stood lean and tall, his handsome features streaked with red ochre. He wore only a breechcloth and a beaded medicine pouch around his neck. On his feet were the porcupine-quill embroidered moccasins I had made for him. The sweat on his body glistened, high-lighting the smooth bronze muscles of his body. My heart swelled with pride.

Pressed tight between my future mother-in-law and Pawho, I followed Quawno, Okemaw, and the other warrior at a discreet distance while Quawno called out repeatedly in a loud, authoritative voice, "People make way. Okemaw, chief of the Standing Elk band of Akwanakai, desires to pass! Make way!"

The crowd parted before them. Following the three walked the fortunate few who considered themselves close enough kin that they could accompany the men to an audience with the Bear Faces. Reaching their destination, the people fanned out in a circle, my family of in-laws just behind Quawno. I stood on my tiptoes to see between heads.

One of the Bear Faces raised a musket, and a loud explosion and a loud explosion shook the ground. The crowd drew back with a gasp. Giant orange-red flames had shot into the sky, followed by a billow of sharp acrid smoke. Over the babble of terrified voices, children cried and infants shrieked. Quawno grabbed for me and, pulling me toward him, enfolded me protectively in his arms.

Wanaga's voice rose above the din. "My Akwanakai people, have no fear. The thunder and fire the Bear Face just summoned from the sky will not harm you. I stand ready, my people, to intercede with the Bear Faces so that no ill may befall you. Hear me," he shouted, "there is no danger!"

The terrified voices began to still. Trembling women picked up their children to quiet their cries.

"My people," Wanaga continued, "the Bear Faces call down the thunder death only upon their enemies. They know me to be a man of wisdom and power and seek me to guide them as they search for the path from Michacoupee to the river of our winter camp. I have promised their chief, Marquette, that I will stay with them to be their guide on this journey and I promise to you that when the Bear Faces have reached the Father of Waters, Misi-ziibi, I will not forget you, my people. I will return as your leader and bring many gifts."

Though Quawno now stood in front of me, I still had my fingers threaded in his strong grip. Peering between his shoulder and that of the other warrior, I saw Wanaga, bedecked in his bear-claw necklace and garish streaks of paint. He stood defiant, feet spread, arms crossed over his chest. On either side of him stood two pale-skinned men, one in a black robe with a large gold cross dangling from his neck, the other dressed in a buckskin tunic and pants with long greasy strands of hair the color of dead leaves. The two White men did indeed look like bears. Coarse, wiry hair sprouted at all angles and covered their faces, so that only their eyes and noses were exposed.

Wanaga spoke to the Bear Faces as he pointed a bony finger towards our family. One of the White men gave an amiable nod in our direction, although it was clear that his gaze surveyed me from head to feet.

Wanaga motioned to Quawno to approach, then he gestured toward me. I shook my head realizing that Wanaga was indicating for me to come forward as well. I forced down the sour liquid that rose in my throat, and held my head high and glared back at him. He met my eyes with the beady-eyed stare of the raven I remembered from so long ago in Grandpa's pine forest. I watched his lips twitch as though he wanted to smile. *You old crow! What evil do you plan now?* I clutched the soft leather of my skirt to stop my hands from trembling, then reluctantly walked forward. When I reached Quawno, he pulled me into an embrace and I buried my head against his chest.

"Quawno," Okemaw said, his face a solemn mask. "I would speak with you."

I shuddered and clung tighter to Quawno. Okemaw cleared his throat and hesitated, struggling for words.

Wanaga spoke up, "Come, Okemaw, let's get on with it!" He jerked his head toward the White men. "The Bear

Faces' tempers will wear thin soon. You have seen their powerful medicine. Would you have them turn it against the Akwanakai because of your hesitance in this matter?"

Okemaw clenched his teeth and silenced Wanaga with a glare. Then, his face softening, he turned to Quawno. "My warrior brother, forgive me, but I... I have no choice. The Bear Faces' power...you have seen its fearsome results. Not even Wanaga's war medicine can stand against men who can summon the thunder from the sky. Wanaga has promised them your betrothed, Chenoa, as a healer to travel with them. Wanaga has praised Chenoa as a woman wise in the arts of healing. All the Bear Faces have suffered many days from a sickness of the belly, so they have need of a healer to travel with them."

Quawno's eyes went wide. "No!" he shouted. "Chenoa is promised as my wife, according to our Akwanakai rites. She is one with our family and clan. Wanaga has no right to offer her up to the Bear Faces."

Okemaw set his lips in a tight line. "Quawno, I must consider the welfare of our people before all else. In order to assure the future goodwill of the Bear Faces we must honor their request for a healer and Wanaga has promised them—"

"And what of him?" Quawno turned his glare to Wanaga. "You always claim your medicine is more powerful than that of any other shaman. Suddenly you cannot heal an ache in the belly?"

Wanaga's lips curled into a sneer showing blackened and yellowed teeth "My charms and amulets are for a warrior, to keep him safe, curse his enemies, and make him invincible in battle. I do not dabble in simple healing."

Okemaw lowered his voice and leaned toward Quawno. "Wanaga assures me that we must help the Bear Faces in this, so that they will leave the Akwanakai in peace. The Bear Faces' journey is too difficult for Teepawn, and Wanaga does have respect for your woman's healing arts. I have his solemn promise that he will bring Chenoa back with him. Surely you will make this sacrifice for your people?"

Quawno drew himself up and stared full into the eyes of the Bear Faces. "Know that this woman is to be my wife!" he shouted in Akwanakai. "No man shall take her!"

Okemaw's shoulders slumped. His eyes fixed on the ground, he seemed to shrink into himself as he said to the warrior at his side, "Seize Quawno."

Immediately, many strong bronze arms encircled Quawno, pinned his arms behind him, and dragged him out of sight, as he struggled and bellowed curses at Wanaga.

Okemaw took a stand before the crowd and proclaimed, "My people, this woman, Chenoa, will accompany the Bear Faces as a healer, and our brother Wanaga will be their guide. This will seal our pact of peace with the Bear Faces. Let us show to these strange people not weakness and dissension among us but only strength and unity."

Okemaw bent and whispered against my ear. "Chenoa, make your people and family proud. Show courage as the Akwanakai healer you have become."

As he stepped back to re-join his group, I took a deep breath, trying to fight back tears. I had to think. *Wanaga has always wanted to be rid of me. I'm the one who knows that he stole Sawahna's necklace from her grave, and he's afraid that I'll tell the others. He wants to separate me from Teepawn and Quawno, and the rest of my family. Once he has me alone, and away from the clan, it will be really easy for him to arrange for me to have an 'accident' or to become deathly ill. He has no intention of letting me return. If I go with Wanaga and the Bear Faces, I will never see Quawno or my family again!*

Oh, Grandmother, I wish you were here to help me...no, I am going to save myself and stay with my family.

I must do this by my own wits. This is my fight to win or lose!

I looked to the crowd of my people who were obviously terrified by the power of the Bear Faces. I could no longer see any members of Quawno's family. They must have followed him when he was taken away. I doubted that I would get any help from the crowd, even though they far outnumbered Wanaga and the White men.

I needed more time and information in order to come up with a plan. Did either of the Bear Faces understand English? I thought I had heard them speaking French, because it sounded like they were talking with clothespins on their noses. But English? Well, I could only try.

I turned to the man that I'd heard Wanaga call Pere Marquette, hoping that, as a priest, he might be more sympathetic than the other Bear Face.

"Chief Marquette," I said, my voice a timid squeak. I stopped and took a deep breath. When I spoke again my voice came out louder, no longer that of Wanaga's "Little Mouse," but now the voice of a strong woman. "I speak English. Do you?"

Father Marquette raised his eyebrows, as though impressed. "Yes, I speak zee Engleesh. But how do you know this Engleesh?"

Quickly I thought of how best to respond to his question. "I was born Iroquois and learned English from White men as a child. But the Akawanakai are my people now." I gestured toward the crowd.

He nodded. "Ah, is good you speak zee Engleesh for my – how you say? - Po-ta-wa-mee is not so good."

I glanced toward Wanaga, who was narrowing his eyes with suspicion. I had to be careful as I knew he understood some English. I had to convince him that I was resigned to my fate.

"Chief Marquette, I will go with you, but I must return when Wanaga does, for I have an old and feeble grandmother I must care for."

"Oh, my child, have no fear. When Wanaga returns at our journey's end, we send you home wiz him wiz zee blessing of our God."

"You are very kind, Chief Marquette."

Wanaga's face relaxed, then he spoke a few words to Marquette in French and turned to leave. As he passed me he bent and hissed against my ear in Akwanakai, "You are wise, my little healer, to be so accommodating. But oppose me and you and your family will suffer. Have no doubt of that!"

I lowered my head as though frightened and nodded. He had a smug smile on his face as he walked away. I let out the breath I'd been holding.

"Chief Marquette, I must ask you some questions so I may know what healing herbs I should bring with me on our journey."

"Of course, my child. Ask what you will."

I hesitated. His answers could be embarrassing to him, but there was no other way.

"You spoke of having a belly sickness. Tell me where you hurt and what the sickness does."

Father Marquette looked away. "Ah, it is hard to put in zee Engleesh." He shrugged and gestured dismissively, as though he could see no way to avoid what must be said. "Zee pain starts in zee belly, making me feel I would bring up food, zen more pain and…." He paused, pursing his lips, as what I could see of his face reddened. He cleared his throat. "Zee food I do keep in my belly runs through my body like water."

I nodded. "And this sickness, is it only you who suffers?"

"No, we all suffer." He gestured toward the stringy haired man at his side and to another Bear Face musket in hand who stood by their canoe as though guarding it.

I was beginning to suspect where Wanaga fit into all this. If I was right, I could use that knowledge to gain my freedom.

"And Wanaga? Does he have the belly sickness?"

"Oh, no. Because he say he have zee sickness when a child, so he say he will not get zee sickness now."

That was not how the "belly sickness" worked. Wanaga was clearly lying and was probably the cause of their sickness. Perhaps it was all part of his devious plan to get me away from my family, so that he could rid himself of me forever.

But how could I prove it? *His medicine pouch! If he is poisoning the white men, he will have the poison herbs there. It is probably hidden in his own canoe.*

I convinced Marquette that I needed Pawho to fetch my medicine pouch from my wigwam, and that only he knew where it was. I figured he was small enough to search through Wanaga's canoe unobserved. Hopefully he would be able to find the medicine pouch. I had to work fast, as the Bear Faces wished to leave at dawn the next day.

It took a while for a messenger to find Pawho, but luckily Wanaga hadn't yet returned. Finally, Pawho approached our circle with head down, his steps hesitant. He brightened a bit when he saw me. I drew him to one side, away from Marquette and Okemaw, so that they would not be able to overhear my instructions.

"Pawho, I need your help, so that I may remain with our people. This is something only you can do."

"You are as a sister to me. Of course I will help you." He threw back his shoulders and stood tall.

I sighed. He was a boy playing at being the brave warrior. What I was going to ask him to do was dangerous, but I had no choice.

"Pawho, I need for you to find Wanaga's medicine pouch and bring it to me. It is probably hidden in his canoe."

Pawho's eyes went wide and he swallowed hard. My eyes filled with tears. What was I asking this child to do? If caught, he would be labeled a thief and have to face Wanaga's wrath.

"Listen, Pawho, I am wrong to ask this of you. Forgive me." I hugged him and whispered against his ear, "Return to your family and say nothing of what I just asked of you."

He pulled away from me and raised his chin, his expression proud and determined.

"No, I will do this! I am not afraid of Wanaga and the Bear Faces!"

Pawho turned and, before I could stop him, disappeared into the crowd.

Sweat beaded on my forehead and ran down my back as I waited, imagining the worst for Quawno's little brother, and for me.

The White men were speaking together in French, crouched down, sketching in the dirt what appeared to be a map. They motioned to Okemaw to join them and, with gestures and words I could not hear, seemed to be making plans for their journey. I glanced at the sun, trying to gauge how long Pawho had been gone. I was terrified that he would be caught, or that Wanaga would return before I could discover what the old devil carried in his pouch.

Just as I despaired that Wanga had captured Pawho, I spotted the boy clutching a leather pouch to his chest and weaving at a run, in and out of the crowd. I let out the breath I'd been holding. Breathing hard, Pawho, a grin on his face, handed me the pouch. I resisted the urge to hug him. I was sure he now considered himself a warrior who had counted coup on his enemy and was too big to be hugged.

"Thank you, Pawho," I whispered. "Make sure you stay out of sight until the Bear Faces leave."

He gave a brisk and solemn warrior's nod and took off for the trees at a run.

I wasted no time digging into the pouch, and it didn't take long to find what I was looking for. I pulled out a smaller leather pouch from within and found that it contained a gray powder. I sniffed it and wrinkled my nose. Its scent was familiar but I couldn't put a name to it. I needed more evidence to identify it as the poison. From the larger pouch I took out a pipe, a small bag of tobacco, and a withered bird's foot. Then I found my proof— I held in my palm a large egg-shaped root, dirt still clinging to it. Raising it to my nose, I realized the gray powder was ground from the root I held.

I remembered now where I had seen and smelled it before. Long ago, I had brought Teepawn the roots of the Mukte berry bush— elderberry Gram had called it— because I thought our people might be able to grow the bush and use its berries for food. Teepawn had warned me that though the ripe berries could be used for food, the roots must not be eaten, for they would cause belly pain, nausea, and the bowels to run.

Just as I stood and motioned to Marquette that I needed to talk with him, Wanaga re-appeared, startling me. He reached out and wrenched his pouch from my grip, scratching my arm as he did so. But I still held the root firmly in my other hand.

"Thief!" he yelled, as he made a move to slap me.

Marquette put a restraining arm against Wanaga's chest and yelled something in French. Wanaga sputtered a reply. I understood none of their words but could well imagine what they were saying.

Father Marquette turned to me, his voice angry. "Wanaga, he say you steal his pouch. He say you will lie to me and say zat zee pouch is yours. You play me for zee fool, woman?"

"No, Chief Marquette, but Wanaga does."

I started to hold up the root I had clutched in my fist. Wanaga made a lunge for it. I stepped back before he could grab it.

"That is mine!" Wanaga roared in Akwanakai. "The woman is a thief!"

I realized that Marquette did actually know a little of our language, as he seemed to understand Wanaga's shouts.

Marquette held out his hand. "Woman, show me what you hold."

"Chief Marquette, this root is why you and your people have had the belly sickness."

Marquette took the root, sniffed it, and then shook his head with distaste. But he shrugged, as though he saw no connection between the root and his illness, then handed the root back to me.

"Don't you see? Wanaga ground this root of the Mukte berry and put it in your food."

Wanaga snorted. "Such nonsense the woman speaks."

Marquette raised his hands and wrinkled his brow, as if to indicate that he didn't understand. Wanaga spoke angrily to him in French for some time. I assumed he was providing himself with an alibi, as well as discrediting me. Then he made a sudden move to grab me, but again Marquette stopped him.

"Woman, you say this root is poison." He jerked his head toward Wanaga. "He says you are lying because you want to make him seem...zee... oh, how zee Engleesh say...zee villain. How am I to know who is thief or who is the one who poisons?"

I pointed to the root Marquette held. "Tell Wanaga to take a bite from that. He won't do it because it will make him sick. What does not come out of his mouth right away will double him over in pain and in time come out his other end."

Marquette seemed to consider my words. He held out the root to Wanaga. "I will believe you if you take a bite from this."

Wanaga laughed, as if Marquette were making a joke.

Marquette's face hardened and he shouted, "Eat it!"

Wanaga stepped back and, making a fluttering motion of dismissal with his hand, said something in French.

Marquette shook his head. "Eat it!" he roared.

Wanaga's color drained from his face. He turned and ran with Marquette's curses in his ears.

That night, I snuggled against Quawno's shoulder. Staring into the fire, I whispered a prayer of thanksgiving to the Great Manitou. Wanaga had disappeared from the camp. I had convinced Father Marquette to take back the kegs of Spirit Water, in return for goods the people could use. Now, a mound of Bear Face trade goods— kettles, cloth, metal knives and axes, even firesticks, lead balls, and powder, so the Akwanakai could defend themselves against their enemies—was ready to load into the canoes. Life was again good.

FOURTEEN

My face lit up when I spied the black walnut tree with its green-husked nuts spread like a carpet beneath it. Walnuts, those were my favorite. Setting down my burden basket, I knelt under the tree and began scooping up handfuls of the ripe nuts. When my basket was filled, I sat beneath the tree and leaned my back against its rough, deep-furrowed trunk. I hadn't eaten since dawn, and hunger rumbled my belly. I took a nut from the basket. Breaking open its tough, green husk, I extracted the hard brown shell and cracked it open with my teeth. I popped into my mouth the sweet nutmeat nestled inside the shell.

Since dawn, Nemisa, Grandmother, and I had been gathering ripe butternuts, acorns, and walnuts. Nemisa had grown tired after only a short time, so at a spot near the riverbank, we left her to sit in the warm autumn sun with four filled baskets of nuts at her side. After agreeing to meet at midday, Grandmother went in one direction to look for nut trees, and I went in the other.

I checked the position of the sun. About an hour remained before I had to return to the riverbank. With my basket already full, I told myself I deserved to waste that hour doing absolutely nothing. I knew that when we returned, I would face a whole afternoon of husking nuts.

The trouble was that those rare moments when I had no chores to do were when thoughts came unbidden, thoughts I didn't want to deal with. I tried to dismiss the memory of Wanaga leading the War Medicine Dance a few days before. I could see him standing there, the tuft of feathers sprouting from his ceremonial headdress, his face garish, one side painted black, the other red. The old man, his reputation only slightly tarnished after the incident at the trade gathering, was howling his medicine war chant to the frenzied war whoops of the warriors. Quawno was one of them. I couldn't bear to see more. I had left the dance then, squeezing through the press of women and children.

Wiping a tear from my cheek, I told myself I should have stayed, if for no other reason than to bid Quawno farewell. We had been quarreling all day over his determination to join Okemaw on a war party bound for Iroquois territory. If only I had stayed at the Medicine Dance, we could have talked, forgiven each other for words spoken in anger, maybe embraced before he left, but now? I gave a loud sniff. Now, maybe I'd never have another chance to—

Springing to my feet, I didn't let myself finish the thought. *Maybe resting here wasn't such a good idea after all. Much better to be busy, less chance to think. I'll find Grandmother and help her fill her remaining baskets.* Placing my burden basket upon my back, I adjusted its strap around my forehead and set off to find her.

A high-pitched, wailing scream pierced the air. Every muscle rigid, I stopped and listened. Fear, like a claw, gripped my stomach. An Iroquois? But, no, it wasn't a war cry. Again the scream sounded. It was coming from the river. Nemisa!

I dropped the basket and took off at a run. Where the path opened onto the riverbank I saw Grandmother clutching Nemisa in her arms and gently rocking her.

Breathless, I dropped to my knees beside them.

"Nemisa, Grandmother! What happened?"

"Wanaga." Grandmother hissed as though his name was a curse.

"But what did he do?"

Nemisa struggled to speak, her voice a halting whisper. "Chenoa, it was as though he appeared from nowhere. And his face. His face… it wasn't the face of a man at all. The beak, those glittering black eyes. The eyes of the raven they were. He came at me, and I knew he meant to…" She covered her face with her hands, and Grandmother rocked her. After a few moments, she was able to talk. "Such pain I felt in my legs, worse than any I've ever felt— like flames burning my skin." She gave a convulsive sob. "Then nothing! I touch my legs now, and I feel nothing. NOTHING! Chenoa, my legs are dead!"

Teeth clenched with rage, I looked toward Grandmother. "Why did he do this to Nemisa? Why, when it's me he hates?"

Grandmother said nothing, only stared at the ground. When she finally spoke, her voice was slow and pained. "Chenoa, Wanaga fears your medicine power. Like any bully, he hesitates to confront an adversary who is his equal, and that, Chenoa, is what you have become. I see now what he plans. Those you love— it is through them that he seeks to destroy your spirit."

My hands flew to my face. "Quawno!" I spoke his name in a strangled gasp.

"Tell her, Nemisa," Grandmother said, "the words Wanaga spoke to you."

Nemisa hesitated, looking toward Grandmother, her eyes pleading.

"No, child, we cannot spare Chenoa. She must know what he said."

Nemisa drew in a deep, troubled breath. "Wanaga said that you must look to me, and you will see Quawno's fate." She smothered a sob. "Quawno will be wounded, though not die, and return from the warpath a cripple, and, like me, Wanaga will cause him to slowly shrivel and die."

Tears streaming down my face, I asked, "Grandmother, is he able to do that?"

Grandmother slowly nodded. "I fear he can."

"But with your medicine power, surely you can do something to stop him?"

"The power is not mine to stop him, Chenoa. It is yours."

I shook my head with confusion. "Mine?"

Grandmother gestured toward the forest shadows. "Here, it is not safe to speak," she whispered. "We will talk of a plan when we return to the wigwam."

Carrying Nemisa's stick-thin body in my arms, I entered the wigwam and laid her upon the sleeping platform. While Grandmother prepared an herbal tea to help her sleep, I sat beside my sister in silence and held her hand. After she had finished the tea and at last began to doze, Grandmother called me to the hearth and bid me sit.

She gazed into the fire without speaking. Impatient with the old woman's silence, I spoke up. "Grandmother, we have to do something! And quickly. Quawno, Nemisa. We must save them!"

Grandmother looked sadly toward the sleeping platform and shook her head. "Ah, Nemisa, poor child. No herb teas or poultices will restore life to her twisted legs. But Quawno? Wanaga's evil has not yet befallen him. He left only two days ago. It will be a half-moon before Okemaw's war party makes any contact with the Iroquois enemy. Surely, Quawno must yet be whole. Yes, for him there might still be hope."

"Grandmother, just tell me what to do. I will do anything."

"Wanaga's power to make evil medicine must be destroyed. Then he cannot injure Quawno, nor will he be able to do any more harm to Nemisa."

"But how do we destroy his power?"

Grandmother stared into the fire. "Sawahna's bones must be returned to the Hill of the Dead," she whispered. "The evil of dishonor must be undone."

"Sawahna's bones are the source of his evil power?"

"The bones of the dead are not evil in themselves, but Sawahna's bones were dishonored. As a vulture feeds upon death, Wanaga's power feeds upon those bones." Grandmother took both my hands in her own. "Forgive me, Granddaughter. Long ago I knew what must be done, but I said nothing. Fear stopped me. I told myself I could counter his medicine with my own." She glanced toward where Nemisa lay sleeping. "But I was wrong, and now I must pay for my cowardice with my granddaughter's life." Her eyes found mine. "I only pray that I shall not lose you as well."

"No, Grandmother, the guilt is mine, not yours. I'm the one who provoked Wanaga to avenge himself upon Nemisa. At the trade gathering, I could have stopped after I discouraged the Bear Faces from taking me, but I didn't. I wanted to humiliate Wanaga, wrestle him to the ground, rub his face in the sand.

"You know, sometimes it would anger me that you refused to confront Wanaga publicly with his crimes. It seemed you always left the battleground without dealing your enemy the deathblow. But, now I understand. Grandmother, you were wise in your restraint. But me? I was foolish. I wanted to make him bleed. I had to have blood vengeance."

"Sawahna the warrior," Grandmother whispered into the fire and nodded.

"I don't understand."

"As a young woman you were...I mean Sawahna was a warrior. When her husband was killed, she took to the warpath for revenge, so consumed by hatred she was."

"But I've never heard of a Akwanakai woman warrior before."

"Always, Sawahna walked her own path. And, for this, she was often hated, yes, but also respected. Winters passed, and she turned from the path of death to the path of the living, the way of healing. Such she remained until the day she died."

"And such I would be, Grandmother. The healer."

"Ah, but Chenoa, I fear you must first be the warrior. You must steal the bones from Wanaga's wigwam."

My lips tightened into a determined line. "Yes. I think I know where Wanaga might have hidden them. I had plenty of time to watch him when I was his prisoner. There was a spot beneath a sleeping platform where I could sometimes see him digging about. He would always carefully position himself so that I couldn't see what he'd hidden there."

"That seems a logical place, Granddaughter. But first we must make a plan to get you into his wigwam. Since he lives alone, he must go out each day for water, perhaps even to hunt. You will have to lie in hiding to wait for that moment. Then, when he leaves, you enter. Remember, Chenoa, your speed in finding the bones may determine your survival. You will have no way of knowing how long he will be gone."

"Shall I bring the bones back here?"

"No! That you must not do. Have no doubt Wanaga will attempt to follow you, not just to recover the bones, but I fear, this time, to kill you. And, my child, he could very well succeed. You cannot risk confronting him with the bones in your possession. Instead, go directly to a spot we shall agree upon and hide them there."

"There's a big black walnut tree," I said, "not far from where we left Nemisa on the riverbank. Two large roots form a loop at its base. I could wedge the box of bones into the opening and camouflage it with dead leaves and branches. No one could ever see a box was hidden there."

"That will do. Then, Granddaughter, return to us."

I patted the hunting knife I had sheathed on my belt. "And if Wanaga tries to stop me, I have this."

"No, Chenoa, you must not confront him in your human form. That is what he will be hoping for. You are your most vulnerable as a human."

"Then how will I fight him?"

"You are the she-panther, Chenoa."

"But I can't change my shape, not really. The panther vision, it was just that, a vision…a dream."

"Granddaughter, there are many realities. And your humanity is but one, your spirit-panther form another. Have no doubt Wanaga will choose to confront you in animal form."

"The raven?"

"No, he knows that, in a physical contest, the raven will lose against the panther. He will choose well a spirit form he believes can destroy you. He can change to any animal form. He is a master of such shape-shifting medicine. This power he perfected long before Sawahna died. Beware, Chenoa, that power will not be weakened by the loss of the bones."

"But how can I possibly become a panther?"

"You told me that, in your vision, your human form no longer existed. You must summon the same power to change your form from the human. Touch the panther necklace. Sing the medicine song Sawahna taught you that night. Promise me, child, you will try. Your life depends on it."

Solemnly, I nodded.

"And if it happens, Chenoa, that you are mortally wounded, die as the panther. Do that, and you will possess, even in your death, a spirit power he can never take from you."

Her black eyes took on a faraway look. "And so it shall be when my time on this earth is to end. I will seek out my wolf sisters, run free with the pack one last time, feel the cold wind ruffling my fur. Teepawn shall die as the she-wolf, not imprisoned in this turtle shell of a human body."

I swallowed hard. I didn't want to die as a panther or a wolf. I didn't want to die as anything. I wanted to live, so that I could be with Quawno. But since I had provoked Wanaga I must now negate his evil medicine. I drew in a deep breath. "I will do what you ask of me, Grandmother."

She embraced me.

"Quawno and Nemisa?" I whispered. "They will live if I do this?"

"Without your panther necklace and Sawahna's bones, Wanaga's power, though not destroyed, will be weakened. Let us pray to the Great Manitou that such is enough, and that they may live. We can only do what we know we must. And hope. When finally Wanaga leaves on another one of his long mystery journeys, that is the time we will return Sawahna's bones to the Hill of the Dead, to a place he will never know."

Tears shone in the old woman's eyes as her gaze rested on me. "And, Granddaughter, if it shall come to pass, that you never again return to us, then I alone will go to the hiding place beneath the black walnut tree. I will bury the bones in the Hill of the Dead. Either way, it shall have ended at last. Sawahna's circle of life and death will be complete."

I watched the sparks flare and crackle as Grandmother added another branch to the fire. "It shall have ended"—those words of Grandmother's wouldn't stop ringing in my ears. *Yes, the burying of the bones would indeed be an end.*

With that act, will I be turning my back forever on Mama, Daddy, Gramma and Grampa? Is it not only Sawahna's bones I'll be laying in the grave, but also the White girl I once was? I remembered something Wanaga had said when he had first captured me, and a disturbing possibility seized me. *With the possession of Sawahna's bones will I at last have the means to return to the twentieth century?* I shook my head to drive away the thought, but it refused to be banished.

I looked hesitantly toward Grandmother, then finally decided to speak. "I remember Wanaga telling me that he had needed three things to bring me to this time—the panther necklace, Sawahna's bones, and my spirit within his power. Soon, in my possession will be all three of these things." My voice trembled. "Could...could it be that I might be able to return to my time and the body that once was mine?"

The old woman took a deep, troubled breath. "I, too, have pondered this. Perhaps that was the true reason I did not speak to you earlier of recovering the bones. Forgive me, Granddaughter, for I had no right to decide the path your spirit must walk. But I could not face losing you."

My face brightened with hope. "Then you think returning to my time is possible?"

"I cannot know for sure. The knowledge lies within Sawahna...within you, Chenoa. But I know it would be dangerous, even with Sawahna's knowledge. The exact time, the place, the manner of your return—all would have to be perfect.

And, if they were not? Who can know the outcome? Death? An undetermined place in time? Or worse still, lost in a void that knows no end?"

I broke into sobs. "But, Grandmother, I don't belong in this time! Look about you. What have I brought upon Nemisa, Quawno, you? Nothing but evil! If I had never come, Wanaga would not be pursuing you like a weasel chases its prey. No, don't you see? It's wrong for me to be here. I know too much of what is to be. I don't want to see the Bear Faces destroy the man who would be my husband and father to my children.

The White Man will ravage my people, the forests, the streams, the animals. Grandmother, as Sawahna, I once died to this time. Sixteen winters ago, I died. Sawahna is dead! DEAD! Let me return to where I have life. Let the child, Becca Morrison, bury Sawahna's bones within the Hill of the Dead."

FIFTEEN

I lay prone in the underbrush and peered between the leaves toward Wanaga's wigwam. Wisps of smoke spiraled from its domed roof. I had lain there, barely moving, for hours. I began to wonder if he was in the wigwam at all. But surely he must be. Someone had to be feeding the fire for it to keep smoking. I shuddered, remembering him as he looked so long ago sitting hunched near the fire, chanting endlessly over his evil amulets.

The sun reached its zenith, then began its downward journey. My muscles ached. My arms and legs had become a mass of itching, burning insect bites. I fought to keep my eyes open, but my mind was slowly numbing. At my elbow, a bumblebee bobbed lazily among a fragrant clump of white clover blossoms, his buzz a lulling hum. The wigwam blurred. Then nothing.

I jerked up my head. How long had I slept? I glanced toward the sun. It was lower, but how much? I wasn't sure. My throat tightened. Could he have left while I had dozed? I looked toward the wigwam. The smoke still spiraled into the fierce blue of the sky.

Then I saw the fur robe covering the doorway pushed aside, and a copper-skinned gnome-like figure came out and, like a forest animal, cautiously sniffed the air before he ventured further into the clearing. I froze, my heart pounding. Wanaga walked toward the forest path, then disappeared from sight, blocked by a thick tangle of bushes. I waited, not daring to breathe. Long moments passed before I began to worm my body through the underbrush. Taking an anxious look around the deserted clearing, I forced myself to stand.

I knew I had to act quickly or I would lose my nerve. I sprinted across the clearing, then shoved aside the fur robe covering the entrance to the wigwam. The familiar rancid stench rose to my nostrils, triggering a rush of memories. I felt a sick fear, almost nausea. Fighting down the sour lump rising in my throat and the trembling in my hands, I forced my eyes to search the dark. I spotted the sleeping platform I had often seen Wanaga digging under. Rummaging beneath it, I found nothing except a nest of mice.

Could it have been another sleeping platform? I searched under the other three. Nothing. Panic pounded a beat in my head. At any moment he could push aside the entrance robe and discover me in his wigwam.

I scanned the walls. My eyes lit on a peculiar bulge above one of the beams. Taking a long branch from the firewood pile, I poked at the bulge, dislodging a section of grass mat that fell to the floor. Then I saw it—Gramma's wooden chest with its rusty clasp, wedged into a niche under the roof.

With the branch, I pried a corner of the box loose from its niche. Lifting the wood bucket by the doorway, I poured out its contents, the water soaking into the dirt floor in a dark, spreading stain. I placed the bucket, rim down, on the sleeping platform and used it as a step stool. Tottering on the bucket's base, I stretched full-length and could just reach the niche.

Moments later, the chest of bones under my arm, I stood outside the wigwam. As my eyes skittered over the clearing, I felt as though a metal band were tightening relentlessly around my chest. No sign of Wanaga. I took off at a run, slowing only when I was deep within the forest. Each step had to be carefully chosen now. My life depended on it—leave no imprint of a moccasin in moist dirt, no broken branches or bruised leaves.

I knelt beneath the black walnut tree and wedged the chest with Sawahna's bones into its looping roots, then covered the roots with dead leaves and weighted them down with a heavy branch. Warily, I scanned the surrounding trees and shadows before setting off on the roundabout route I had planned back to Grandmother's wigwam.

It was nearing dusk when I stopped on the edge of a small clearing to rest. As I leaned back against the trunk of an oak, a strong musky odor rose to my nostrils. My body went rigid. Stepping away from the tree, I saw long white gashes scraped in the bark. Grizzly!

With a screaming roar, the massive bear rose up from the underbrush. The oak's branches were too high to climb, but nearby a young maple had a low hanging branch. I sprang for it as the bear lunged for me. Grabbing a branch, I pulled myself up to the lowest crook of the tree. I reached for another limb and heaved myself up one more notch. The bear stood beneath me, his snout open in a cavernous snarl, saliva dripping in a foaming froth from his yellow fangs. He gave an enraged roar and, with his huge forepaw, swiped at my leg. I screamed as the curving talons gashed long, red streaks in my calf. Shimmying up the narrow trunk, I clung to a spindly branch that placed me barely out of reach of the swinging claws.

Grandmother's words rang in my head, "Die as the panther, Chenoa. Do that, and you will possess, even in your death, a spirit power he can never take from you."

I clutched the panther pendant and my medicine song rose in a quavering wail. The song washed over me in cooling dark waves, pulling me deep, deep within. My pain and fear were numbed. I was floating and free now. Physical sensations ceased to be. A trance, death-like, gently swallowed my human form.

My panther mother was licking me. As I felt the rasp of her coarse tongue I sensed the change in my limbs, my whole body. The human was no more. The she-panther had been re-born.

Full-grown, my coat sleek and golden, I crouched upon the limb, every muscle tensed for the pounce, my long tail rhythmically slashing the air. My yellow eyes glowed with hatred. With a piercing scream, I sprang, my paw slashing the bear from his ear to his muzzle. The bear flung my panther body against a tree trunk with one mighty swipe.

Emitting an anguished cry, the bear staggered for a moment on his hind legs. Blood was gushing from his torn eye socket and dripped onto the dark fur of his belly. He sank to all fours, his massive head swaying with the agony of pain and sudden blindness.

I lay dazed at the base of the tree. Slowly, the earth, the forest came into focus. The scent of the bear's blood wafted to my nostrils and I snarled my fury. I staggered and stood. In confusion, I watched the trees until they stopped spinning. I looked toward the bear. He was swiping blindly at the air with his massive paws. I hoped that I was not close enough to be hit. Then he paused, sniffing the air. With a bellow, he spun toward me and slowly advanced.

Roaring defiance, I bolted away into the underbrush. Each step was a flying leap, faster and faster, until I merged with the wind, the ground blurring beneath me. I sprang into a tree. Crouching tense within its crook, I called to the first star of the night my song of victory.

* * *

I awoke to a fire in my calf. I tried to raise my head and suddenly lurched to one side. Grabbing the nearest limb, I clung to it for balance. The ground was far beneath me, the height of a man and more. I fought to make sense of where I was and why. A bear had treed me. I remembered that as reality. The pain and the long gashes on my leg were evidence that I hadn't dreamt the grizzly bear—but the rest?

I swung to the ground. I held myself rigid from the pain in my leg and side. Raising my buckskin shirt, I looked for the source of the sharp, shooting pains. My ribs on one side were blue with bruises. I remembered the dream. The bear had thrown the panther against a tree trunk after she had lashed its face.

I looked down at my hand and gasped. Bits of dried blood crusted my fingers, showing brown under my fingernails. Dissolving into sobs, I sank to the ground and tried to wipe the dried blood from my hands onto the dew-soaked grass. No, there had to be a rational reason for the dried blood. A wound from the bark, a sharp twig, anything but the answer the dream suggested.

When I entered the wigwam Grandmother arose stiffly, her movements uncharacteristically slow and feeble. She opened her arms to me. "My granddaughter," she said, "at last, you have come."

I ran to her, and we clung in an embrace. "There was a bear. He would have killed me. But, I…I, oh, Grandmother, I don't even know anymore what's real and what's a dream."

"Granddaughter, it is real, all of it. The she-panther has vanquished our enemy. This morning a woman ran through the village crying out, "Potowok has found Wanaga wandering the forest, blinded. Attacked by a panther he was. One eye ripped right from its socket."

I gave a shuddering cry and sank to my knees. Grandmother knelt beside me. Once I was calmer she asked, "The bones?"

"I hid them beneath the black walnut, as we planned."

A faint, wailing moan sounded from Nemisa's sleeping platform.

With alarm, I looked to Grandmother.

"Nemisa is dying," the old woman said softly.

"No, that can't be! But the bones? Now that Wanaga no longer possesses them, won't she recover?"

Grandmother slowly shook her head. "Her body is consumed by fever, her legs dead. The earth holds nothing but pain for her now. What evil Wanaga did to Nemisa cannot be undone."

Grandmother rose and I followed. Nemisa, her face glossy with fever, lay on her robe. I knelt beside her and took her hand. "My sister, you cannot die. You have a life yet among us. You have your stories. The children." I forced myself to smile through my tears. "Ayah, Nemisa, I am sure, you shall live to be the wise old one who carries in her head all the history of our band. Why, you will probably outlive me." I gave Nemisa's feverish hand a squeeze. "But first you have to find the will to fight death."

Nemisa struggled to speak. I had to lean close to hear her. "When my legs died, my spirit sought death, also. I see my sister, Chenoa, returned alive from the evil one... now I can go."

"No!" I sobbed and pressed my cheek against Nemisa's. "I won't let you die! It is fitting that I be the one to die. I caused this!"

Grandmother stroked my back. "No, my granddaughter. Nemisa must leave us. Her time for her final journey has come. Soon, my time must come also." She tenderly caressed Nemisa's cheek. "Perhaps, my little granddaughter, it is best we should journey the path of the Milky Way together."

My tear-blurred eyes found Grandmother's in the shadows. "Don't leave me, Grandmother. Not you, too!"

"Chenoa, do not mourn me, for now I am at peace. I have accepted that you have chosen another path than the

Akwanakai, that you shall return to the Bear Faces. And Nemisa and I, we also have chosen another path, though one not of this earth."

Grandmother walked to the wall and pulled a leather-bound bundle from a niche. She handed it to me. "Within this bundle are your Bear Face clothes, the leggings, the shirt, the moccasins. You must wear them when you return to your time. All must be as it was that day when Wanaga kidnapped you. Come now, we must make preparations, but first I must care for your wounds."

After she had applied a healing salve to my leg, she glanced toward Nemisa. "The child nears death and our time here is short. I have sung my medicine song, prayed to the Great Manitou. Helping you to return to your people is all that remains undone. I understand now exactly how it must be accomplished, this journey through time."

She let out a deep troubled breath. "You were right, Chenoa. It is better that Becca return the bones to the sacred Hill of the Dead. Then Wanaga can never find them. For without Sawahna's bones and the panther necklace, the power to travel through time will no longer exist. Such medicine is evil and was never meant to be."

Nemisa moaned softly. With a spreading ache in the center of my chest, I looked sadly toward my sister. I started to put on my old clothes, first pulling the dirty t-shirt over my head. But it was too small and I struggled to arrange it over my grown woman's body. I suddenly realized what a different person I had become in my years with the Akwanakai.

"Grandmother, is it only my spirit that can return to the body I once occupied?"

"I do not understand your words, Granddaughter."

"Would it be possible for Nemisa to enter Becca's body instead?"

"Aiee, I do not know. There are so many dangers, even for you."

"But, Grandmother, Nemisa faces death, anyway. Isn't the chance worth it? Her spirit would at last have a body whole and strong. A chance to truly live." I took both Nemisa's hands in my own and said, "Nemisa, I can give you a life... a healthy body. Please, take my gift."

Confusion and pain mingled on Nemisa's face. "But, what of you, Chenoa? You need to return to your own people. I cannot take this from you."

My eyes filled with tears. "I have a life among the Akwanakai. Quawno will survive, I feel that strongly now."

Grandmother slowly shook her head. "Granddaughter, I see such sorrow ahead if you remain here. What of your knowledge of what is to be? The two peoples you love— the Akwanakai, the Bear Faces? Think how your spirit will be torn apart when you must watch the one destroy the other."

"Possibly there can be another outcome. Perhaps my knowledge can help the Akwanakai turn aside their fate."

"No, Chenoa, you can never change that which is to be. Remember your vision quest. The she-panther could not stop the destruction of her kind."

"But, Grandmother, I am the healer, as Sawahna was the warrior. Chenoawockquai, you called me, 'Woman who brings forth life.' I know there are those descended from our people who live now in Becca's far away time. Their ancestors somehow survived, escaped the Bear Faces, lived to cherish and preserve our ways, and to give the gift of life to their children and grandchildren for generations. Perhaps I, in some way, can help to bring about their survival. Grandmother, I must fulfill my vision. My place must be with my Akwanakai people, that the sacred circle of my life may be completed."

Grandmother looked sadly toward Nemisa and brushed a fever-soaked strand of hair from her eyes. "And, where, my poor child, shall your circle of life be completed. Here? Or, in Becca's time, so far away?"

Nemisa, her face pinched with pain, looked toward me. "But how can I do as you ask and go to this place? I will be a stranger among those who will call me daughter, granddaughter, friend. My life among them will be a deception. I can never be you, the child you once were. Who would I be? I do not even know. Would I be this child, Becca Morrison, you've so often told me of? But then what of my spirit, Nemisa's spirit? Would she be no more? And, loss of spirit, is that not truly death? A death far more final than death of the body?"

"My sister, the spirit of Becca is not dead." I touched my chest. "Becca still dwells within me, and so she will always. And also Nemisa will live on, but in the body of Becca Morrison."

Nemisa's face tightened in a spasm of pain. When it had passed, she continued in a halting whisper. "But, Chenoa, the deception to your Bear Face family? I cannot live such a lie. And, surely they would know I am not their child. You have taught me a little of the Bear Face tongue, the picture words, told me tales of your far away life, but I would be ignorant of so much."

Some spirit returning to her voice, Grandmother spoke up. "A blow to the head, it makes a person forget. Chenoa has told us that when she awoke to our time, she had a memory of Wanaga having struck her head before he kidnapped her. That would explain the blanks in memory. You would have to 're-learn' that which Becca once knew."

Nemisa resolutely shook her head. "But, Chenoa, the deception. Is your kin ever to know the truth of where you really are?"

"Nemisa, you are a singer of songs," I said. "Once you scratched into the dirt the picture words of your own song. When the child, Becca, has grown to a woman perhaps you will find a way to sing my song and yours, also."

"But how can your kin ever understand your song? Such a strange, unbelievable mystery it is, this weaving together of faraway times and lives."

"Remember, Nemisa, when you first told me of your spirit song. You said, none can truly understand another's song, but still you needed to sing it, just to say that you once lived, loved, laughed, cried, walked this earth. My spirit sister, though my kin will never truly understand, perhaps someday you can sing my song before the campfires of my Bear Face people. Tell my kin that the Akwanakai woman, Chenoawockquai, never stopped loving them, even though she chose to walk the path of another people and another time. No, Nemisa, they will never understand, but it will be enough that they hear my song."

Later that day, Grandmother and I stood within a clearing. Nemisa, lay at our feet upon the forest's carpet of leaves, her chest barely moving. I had led them to this place, for my spirit had told me this clearing was the same location where my body lay in the twentieth century. Grandmother had said that, as much as possible, all must be how it had been on the day Wanaga kidnapped me. I held the chest containing Sawahna's bones under one arm. Nemisa was clothed in the tattered jeans, t-shirt, and sneakers I had worn five winters earlier. Although the clothes were those of a child, they hung loose on her emaciated body.

Grandmother turned to me and said, "Remove your panther necklace and place it around Nemisa's neck. The one whose spirit is to be transferred to another body must wear the necklace." Anxiously, she glanced down at Nemisa. "Quickly, Chenoa! We must hurry, before her body dies in this time, and her spirit departs from us."

Placing the necklace around Nemisa's neck, I said, "Grandmother, I know I must accompany Nemisa back to my Bear Face time, or the medicine will not work, but you?

There's too much danger. If Nemisa and I are lost forever..." I hesitated, my voice beginning to quaver. "Why must you risk such a fate also?"

"It is only between us both, Chenoa, that we possess the medicine knowledge and power to accomplish travel through time. It is necessary I go. Now, kneel with me. Put the chest between us. We will all join hands and—"

"Aiee! I just remembered...my glasses." My hands flew up to my face. "You said all must be as it was that day. They were broken, but the frame was still intact. I put one of the lenses in my medicine bag, but the frame was with my clothes. I'll run back to the wigwam and get it."

"No, there's no time. See, Nemisa's breathing grows shallower. Your glasses must remain in our time. Now, quickly, take Nemisa's hand." Grandmother opened the chest. "Place your other hand upon the bones. Look deep within your spirit, Chenoa, for only you and Sawahna know the medicine chant that will bring us to the future time."

"But I can't remember the words I used to chant to summon Wanaga. In the pines, it was always as though someone else sang through my lips."

"Sawahna is one with you. Her knowledge is yours also, Chenoa. Remember when you sought to become the she-panther? You sank deep within yourself. Seek out that sacred place again. Sawahna awaits you there."

I closed my eyes. For a long moment I sat in silence, then the soft wavering trill of a medicine song rose to my lips.

When I heard Sawahna's voice die out on the wind, I slowly opened my eyes. Before me, on a bed of pine needles lay my own body. Becca, the child of almost thirteen, was dressed in a dirty gray t-shirt and jeans, her pale, thin face strangely naked without her glasses. A huge lump was raised on her forehead. Her cheek was bruised and swollen. Upon her chest lay the panther necklace. Silent tears streaming down my cheeks, I reached out in love to touch the child I had once been, then gave a start, as the child opened her eyes and met my gaze.

A shout sounded in the distance. "Becca. BECCA!"

I felt my throat tighten. It was Gramma's voice.

Grandmother put her hand on my arm. "We must hurry. They search for the child. Take from Nemisa the necklace. It remains yours, and we shall need it in order to return to our time."

Grandmother knelt and kissed Nemisa's cheek. "Farewell, my granddaughter. Sawahna's bones I leave for you to bury in the sacred Hill of the Dead." Her eyes cast about the clearing and lit on a large fallen limb. "I will place the chest beneath that limb over there, hidden so that none but you may find it. Chenoa and I will remain close to the bones, so that our medicine, which enables us to return, will still work."

Nemisa slowly nodded. "I will return the bones, Grandmother, to their rightful place." She raised herself to a sitting position and embraced the old woman. Her voice was tense with emotion. "I will never forget you, Grandmother, my people, the Akwanakai. I promise you this!"

Grandmother returned the embrace. "A new life, a new body you have now, my granddaughter. May you walk your new path in honor and love, until the Great Manitou calls you to your last journey." She gently but firmly extricated herself from Nemisa's arms. "I go now to hide the bones. I leave you to bid Chenoa farewell." The old woman rose and taking the chest walked toward the fallen tree limb.

Nemisa and I clung in a silent embrace.

"Becca! BECCA! Now, where can that child be?" Gramma's voice was closer now. "Papa, do you think something could've happened to her?"

"Aw, no, Anna," said Grampa. "Figure she's just off playing somewheres. You know how wrapped up Becca can get in her make-believe games."

Her voice urgent, Grandmother called from the opposite side of the clearing, "Hurry, Chenoa, we must leave soon."

"Nemisa, I love you," I whispered. No other words would come.

Nemisa met my eyes. "And know, my sister, I love you."

"Come quickly," Grandmother whispered in a desperate hiss. "The Bear Faces are nearing."

I kissed Nemisa's cheek and made a move to stand.

Nemisa, her eyes moist with tears, reached out to touch my hand. "Spirit Sister, I shall sing your song."

I fought tears as I whispered, "As I will sing your song, Nemisa, so that our people may not forget you."

Grandmother grasped my arm. "Come, Granddaughter, the spirit bonds between your Bear Face kin and yourself are too strong. They will see you in your Akwanakai form as once you saw Wanaga. This must not be."

Tears now streaming unchecked down my cheeks, I allowed Grandmother to lead me from the clearing. When we were within a thick wall of pines, I heard Gramma's voice and stopped to listen.

"Here, Papa! Over here. I found her! But, oh my God! She's been hurt. Her head's bleeding. Oh, Becca!"

"Is she conscious, Anna?"

"Yes, yes! See, she's opening her eyes."

I smothered a sob into my hand. "Please," I whispered, "I just want to see Gramma and Grampa one more time. I won't let them see me. I'll peer between the branches and... just for a moment."

Firmly, Grandmother embraced me. "No, Chenoa. Look no longer behind you. Now you must look only forward... forward to this life path you have chosen."

Author's Note

Native American culture and spirituality have been a life-long interest. During my years as an elementary school teacher and throughout the raising of five children, I always found some time to imagine the lives and to research the history of Native American tribes. I hope **Spirit Sister, I Sing Your Song** shows the reverence I feel.

www.ingramcontent.com/pod-product-compliance
Lightning Source LLC
Chambersburg PA
CBHW051251250626
47155CB00009B/3257